CW01664743

Best Things in Life

# WALK THE LINE

STACEY SOLOMON

Walk the Line
ISBN # 978-1-78651-327-4

Interior text design by Claire Siemaszkiewicz
Totally Bound Publishing
Stacey Solomon Management: Total Artist Management



Published in 2016 by Totally Bound Publishing, Newland House, The Point, Weaver Road, Lincoln, LN6 3QN, United Kingdom.



Totally Bound Publishing is a subsidiary of Totally Entwined Group Limited.

# WALK THE LINE

# Dedication

Zachary and Leighton – The loves of my life. Driving me to succeed in all I do. I love you more than you'll ever know!

Mummy, Daddy, Bubba Solomon – The best parents anyone could wish for guiding me strong and steadily through life! Without you I wouldn't exist! What a terrible thought! Haha.

Jemma and Matthew Solomon – Love u bro and sis always there when I need you and supporting everything I do!

Warren Askew – For being the best manager in the world/ best friend/loser inspiring me and pushing me to be the best that I can be. Always believing in everything that I do! Making it happen no matter what! Nothing is impossible.

Hayley, Harvey, Darcey, Winter and Grayson – I love you all, my extended family.

My Besties (you know who you are)
Love you girls.

# 1

I stared at Blake standing there on my doorstep, my vocal cords frozen, my heart thudding like no one's business. Oh my word, if I wasn't careful I'd faint from shock. Blinking didn't make him go away, and usually, when I was dreaming, blinking was the way to go—it woke me up and I'd realise I'd been somewhere else other than reality. My daydreaming really did have a hold on me. But I wasn't daydreaming. There he was, suitcase sitting on the ground beside him, his face expressing hope and fear and the expectation of rejection.

"Oh, oh, oh!"

That was hardly what I'd planned to say if I saw him again, but it was all I could get out. My mind had gone AWOL on me, leaving me to fend for myself in the minefield I'd been thrust into.

*Come back and rescue me, brain!*

Aretha Franklin's voice answered me instead, singing *Rescue Me,* and I struggled to make the earworm go away. Now was not a good time to start dancing to her fabulous song.

"Well?" he said, raising his eyebrows like he always did.

I'd missed that. Missed *him.*

Then I squealed in true Lola fashion, the enormity that he was really here hitting me suddenly. The certainty of the moment slapped me on both cheeks, and they flared hotly as I worked my mouth to stop another mad noise coming out. I was conscious of sounding like a deranged monkey.

I stepped back. He walked inside and dropped his suitcase on the floor. It made a clattering sound and scooted forward on its little wheels. It came to a stop in the middle of the hall, and I stared at it, still dumbfounded.

He closed the door, and all the while I held my breath, wanting him to ravish me senseless and erase the past month and more away. There was so much that needed to disappear—emotions, thoughts, my reasons for leaving him in New York. And there was so much to talk about. I'd had no preparation for this, and I was totally out on a limb.

My chest hurt—everything I felt for him had curled up into a ball there, tight and protected, a secret only I knew. If I could find the words to share my feelings I would, but his surreal manifestation had rendered me senseless and—

"Well..." I managed, that one word a choked whisper. "You're...here."

What a silly thing to say. Of course he was here, but perhaps I'd just needed to say it to make it real. The last message I'd got from Blake prior to him being here right now was '*So, in answer to your question asking how much more time I need, I'm almost there, Herman. Listen, I have to go. I'll let you know my answer soon.*'

I'm almost there... I thought he'd meant that he was nearly at the point of finding his answer, which I hoped would be that he couldn't be without me and we should start all over again, putting the past behind us. Oh… That would be delightful, all my Christmases rolled into one. A gigantic present, one I'd treasure for the rest of my life.

"Yes," he said. "I'm here. With my answer."

"Oh my goodness…" I backed into the wall, bumping my hip on the kitchen doorjamb. *Ow.* I might need the wall for support sometime in my immediate future if what he'd come to say was negative. If it was, could I slide down to the floor with grace if he told me to get lost and never darken his life again? Could a woman appear elegant, slumped in a heap in her pyjamas and terry-towelling dressing gown, crying her eyes out and begging for another chance? Was scrunched-up tissue ever a good look?

*Er, no. Get a grip on yourself!*

Now he was standing in my hallway, his presence filling the air and making me vibrate all over—it brought home to me how much I loved him. Yes, I'd missed him while we'd been apart—it had been an absolute nightmare, horrible—but conjuring his face in my head wasn't the same as seeing it for real. Remembering how the atmosphere changed while he was around wasn't the same as *feeling* it.

*I need to pinch myself really hard.*

"What's…?" I'd been about to ask what his answer was but stopped myself. "You said," I began again, my breathing going all skew-whiff, my pulse thudding hard in my throat. "You said you were almost there."

"And I was. At the time of that message I was in a taxi." He flexed his hands in and out of fists, keeping his arms at his sides as though fighting off the urge to lift them and pull me into a hug.

Or maybe I just wanted it to be that.

*Hug me, hug me, hug me…*

"I…" I fiddled with the front of my robe, crossing it more comfortably over my chest then clutching it at my neck with one hand. My subconscious at work? Creating a barrier over my heart so it was protected and wouldn't get broken?

*Oh, stop it with the dramatics and ask him what he's going to do.*

"What's your answer?" I blurted.

He took a step closer, appearing bigger than he was, a giant version of himself that I could be pulled into a hug by, protected and soothed.

My legs weakened.

*Don't you give up on me now. Keep me upright, oh pins of mine.*

"My answer…" He took another step closer. "Is that I…" Another step, so he was inches away from me. "Can't live without you."

A strangled sound popped out of my mouth, and I clamped my lips together. I knew it. He'd said he couldn't live *with* me, and I could hardly blame him. I'd flown away from him without telling him the truth about me—that I was famous here—and left him to find out for himself. Oh, the reasons for me doing that had been valid to me at the time, they'd made perfect sense, but I should have stayed, told him to his face, and watched the dice fall where they had a mind.

"You don't look too happy about that," he said.

A frown streaked across his forehead. I hated that it was there—that once again I'd put one there. I searched my mind for something funny to say to make that frown disappear but all that floated through my head was Aretha doing her thang.

He lifted a hand to rub at his brow. "Have you changed your mind about us? Has being apart given you a different perspective?"

His body heat seemed to shimmer between us, and warmth spread up my chest to my neck, flouncing up past the tight lock of my dressing gown to splash all over my face. He really was *right there*, all manly and beautiful, his lips there for the taking if I had the courage to lean forward a bit and press mine to them.

*To feel his mouth on mine would be Heaven.*

*Kiss him. Go on, kiss him until you can't breathe.*

"It's you who's got a different perspective," I said.

The body language signals he was giving me were all wrong for what he'd said. If you could live without someone and you believed you'd made the right decision about that, why stand there looking as though you were lost and didn't know what to do?

I got the sense that he wanted to kiss me too. Perhaps he needed one of those last snogs, where we cried all the way through it then he moved away, our arms stretched between us, fingers entwined, until he took that final step back and we lost touch except for our tearful eye contact.

*Have I gone into my daydream world and haven't realised it yet? I sound like I want us to star in a soppy movie or something.*

If he kissed me now, I'd never want it to end.

*I should have told him who I was when I stood at that New York apartment door. I should have blabbed it all out then taken the consequences.*

"My perspective is exactly the same as it was before you left New York, Herman."

*Don't use that pet name. Not now. It belongs in the past.*

I choked out a smidgen of a laugh. Or it might have been a sob. "So you've always not wanted to be with me?"

"What?" He frowned harder. "I don't understand."

"I don't either." I smiled, my lips wobbling, treacherous eyes filling.

"Shall I go?" He jerked his head to one side, indicating the door.

Go? If I said yes I'd be insane! My goodness, I wanted him to stay forever.

"No!" I flashed one hand out to grab his coat in my fist.

He stumbled and his body pressed to mine, our mouths inches apart. The sexual chemistry was rife, but was that only my wishful thinking? Something felt only on my part?

"Whoa." He kept his hands by his sides.

*Touch me!*

"Don't go." What was it with the song titles tonight? The tune by the Hothouse Flowers trundled through my head. "Um…" I released his clothing then patted the material down, horrified that I'd made such a faux pas and revealed that his answer had left me needy. "I'm sorry. I'm making this hard for you."

He glanced down at his midsection. "Uh, yeah."

"Huh?" I noticed a twinkle in his eye. *Oh…! Well, that's a bit saucy, isn't it?*

I blushed, my cheeks hot and itchy. I covered them with my hands, stifled by his proximity, needing fresh air and space yet wanting to be swaddled and cosseted by him at the same time. My emotions swirled and I drowned in a wash of 'Take me, take me. Walk away now while I'm still relatively calm. No, take me!'

The voices in my head were on a roll.

"What's going on, Charlotte?"

Oh, he was being serious now, going back to the use of my proper name. I wanted to chant 'Herman, Herman, Herman!' but refrained, thinking it might come off as more than a little bizarre. Like I was cracking up inside.

"I could ask you the same question," I whispered—and kicked myself because, ugh, we were going around in circles, skating the real issue, when really, wasn't it better to rip the plaster off at warp speed and suffer the instant, sharp, stinging pain all at once?

He looked at me, his darling face displaying such confusion. I'd bet mine mirrored it. It felt as though some wires had been crossed, getting all jumbled like spaghetti. Not giving myself time to talk myself out of it, I reached out to cup his face. And I was undone. A zillion memories bombarded me—our excursion around The Big Apple in a taxi, me eavesdropping on him while stuck in a bush outside Gianni's restaurant, our time on the beach at The Hamptons when we'd flirted with the waves and I'd laughed my head off, feeling so free and…*me.*

"This is driving me crazy." He rested his hand over my ear to cover it and gazed down at me with so much love that he had to be having a hard time finally letting me go—*us* go.

*Oh my goodness me…*

My legs decided they didn't need muscles and bones and went to jelly on me. My knees jolted, and I was a puppet without strings. I swallowed the huge lump that had made itself uncomfortable in my throat, and shallow-breathed, trying to stop myself from crying.

"I said I can't live without you, but it seems you don't feel the same about me anymore." He stroked my cheekbone with his thumb.

I blinked. "Pardon?"

"I said—"

I breached the tiny space between our faces, clamping my lips to his in a kiss so passionate, so *Iloveyoupleasedon'tleavemeagain,* that my head went giddy. He sank into me, kissing me back. Then he pushed me harder against the wall, tunnelling his hand into my hair, sliding his other to the small of my back. I wanted every part of him close to me, and all the while I tried to process what he'd said and how I'd misheard him the first time.

He broke the kiss to murmur, "I've missed you so much. I thought…thought you didn't want me. I can't… I don't want to ever be away from you again."

And his words finally sank in, swimming through my body and mind, singing a feisty hallelujah, Gospel style. The word hallelujah reverberated, giving me the warm fuzzies and threatening to send me into a faint that was fit for a woman in the 1800s.

"You don't want this?" he asked, frowning again. "How can you kiss me like that and not want me? Explain, so I can understand."

I frowned back. *The head shake. He thinks…* "No! I mean yes, I want this. I was just—"

He cut me off with another kiss. Suddenly I couldn't get enough of him—need and want, emotions and love and desperation all combining into a big, heavy lump that crashed into me, a wrecking ball intent on knocking me off my feet. My legs still didn't see the need for muscles and bones, and my arms had decided on much the same, so I let Blake hold me up and kissed and kissed and kissed until I wrenched my mouth away to gasp for air.

"I love you," I panted, elated and bubbling up inside like Coke exploding from a shaken can. I lowered my forehead to his chest. The warmth of his body and his scent billowed upwards. "And I'm so bloody sorry. For everything. Me leaving, you having that accident at work… If I hadn't left maybe you'd have been concentrating better."

"No," he said into my hair. "No. None of it's your fault. We both messed up."

His ragged breathing inflated his chest, mine rising to meet it with every inhalation. I raised my head to look at him, and for the longest time we stared, me still unable to believe he was here.

"Where's your bedroom?" He touched his forehead to mine. "I need…you."

And I needed him. More than he'd ever know.

# 2

We kissed our way up the stairs, pausing halfway when passion took over completely. There—me on one step, Blake on the other below—he undid the knot of my robe belt. Him doing that made me lightheaded enough that I had to steady myself by clamping hold of his shoulders. The last thing I needed was to swoon all the way down the stairs. Then he pushed the dressing gown off my body. It pooled around my feet.

It was one of those moments where I again wished I were a sexier woman. My fuzzy warm pyjamas were ideal for cosying up on the sofa while watching TV, but in a situation like this I could have done with owning something a little daintier. Maybe a soft, wafty chemise that floated around my body, making me look alluring and desirable. Or a two-piece—boy boxers and a vest top with shoelace straps.

Blake didn't appear to mind my current outfit. He gazed up and down my body, a faint smile tweaking his lips. I didn't feel that he was laughing at what I was wearing, more that it was what he'd expected, what he might have envisioned me in if he'd thought about me in *that* way while we'd been apart.

He tugged down my bottoms, kissing me. I stepped out of them then scuffed them to one side. As I walked up the stairs backwards, I smiled at him. Then I took his hand and led him onto the landing, where he removed my top then threw it to the floor. I'd lost my self-consciousness in his company while I'd been in New York, but now it was back—not full-blown but definitely there. It was as though the uncertainty of the past few weeks had zipped me back to my old self somewhat, and all those unanswered questions had brought with them some of the awkwardness of a first love-making session.

*It's Blake. No need to feel like this...*

I attacked his trouser button and zip, divesting him of his clothing so we were both naked and vulnerable. But vulnerable wasn't the right word. Equal was more like it, on a level footing, the pair of us the same. My courage returned as I stared at his body and remembered exactly what I'd been missing. It wasn't just his body either, but him, his personality, everything that he was.

He brushed his fingertips over my shoulders, and I held my breath, closed my eyes, and focused on what he was doing. I was hyperaware—the hairs on my neck and body lifted, goosebumps scattered all over me, and my need tickled, threatening to grow and overtake every other sense.

Our breathing sounded heavy and fractured, loud in the quiet, and it was like those breaths were right inside my head, amplified a thousand times. An aura seemed to surround us, gentle and caressing, creating a private bubble belonging only to us. He had such a light touch that I could barely feel it, yet at the same time I could. He pressed his palms to my collarbone and steered me backwards.

I read his eyes like a compass, trusting him to guide me in the right direction. In my peripheral vision I saw my bedroom doorway and a tumble of discarded clothing on the bedroom floor from where I hadn't had the heart or energy to put them in the laundry hamper. My bed was covered with a scrambled heap of quilt and pillows, evidence of my restless nights.

I made it to the foot of the bed, where I closed my eyes to enhance my senses, and it seemed like a million years had passed since he'd arrived at my front door. Years I didn't mind spending—I'd spend another million with him. I could stand here forever like this.

If a pin dropped I'd hear it. If a gust of wind shoved at the branches of a tree a mile down the road I'd hear it. In that second I was so attuned to life, to *being*, that it was a somewhat shocking revelation that I could even *become* this sensitive. Whenever Blake was around I was taken to another world.

"Oh," I whispered.

He placed one hand on my cheek, the other on my chest, kissing me gently. It was unhurried and mesmerising. Time stilled, holding me in a cocoon of perfect suspension. He kissed on, each peck almost imperceptible, giving me electrical jolts, and I scrunched my toes and fingers.

I gasped again, loudly this time, the air was cold at the back of my throat, drying it out. I swallowed, clenching my hands into fists, digging my nails into my palm, hard enough, I knew, to leave four crescent imprints on each. My arms shook with my effort to remain still, then my legs followed suit. I bit my bottom lip hard, holding my breath.

I looked up to see his lips were plump, his cheeks flushed. He pressed me down until I sat with relief on the end of my bed. I shook, riddled with emotion, clamping my teeth together so they didn't chatter.

Then he gently urged me backwards on the mattress, where I scooted towards the headboard. I shivered, the good kind, my skin chilling now that he wasn't standing so close.

Gazing at me the way he was—eyes hooded, mouth slightly parted—sent me dizzy. I stared back at him and listened to my heartbeat as it thudded dully then picked up pace until one throb blended into the next. I exhaled through pursed lips, the air juddering. With my hands on the mattress either side of me, fingers splayed, I resisted scrunching the sheet into them. I needed something to hold on to, something to ground me so I didn't float away, but I'd wait until I could hold on to him instead.

He climbed onto the bed, the mattress dipping with his muscled weight, my tummy doing somersaults. Settling by my side, he propped himself up on one elbow and looked down the length of me. His closeness brought on a fresh burst of expectation. Perhaps he'd kiss me again.

I tucked one arm behind my head so I could watch him. I wondered how he saw me—I saw myself very differently, I was sure. He'd told me before that he thought I was beautiful, and I believed that to him I truly was.

We belonged here, like this, together in that special way.

We kissed, emotions on full display, every bit of me raw and bare. He tucked his hands beneath me, holding me tight. My *self* seemed to part from my body, and for a few ecstatic seconds I was suspended above us, looking down at our wonderful reunion.

With my head spinning and senses scattering, I floated back into my body, which was loose-limbed, pliant and wrung out. I controlled my breathing as Blake brushed some of my hair from my face, tucking it behind my ear then tracing the shell of it. Then he drew a line along my jaw until his fingertip came to rest on my mouth.

"Don't say anything," he whispered. "Not yet. Just…let us be."

Blake rolled away, taking me with him so I nestled into his side. He covered his eyes with his forearm, his breathing returning to its usual pace. What was he seeing inside his mind? What emotions was he feeling? I put my hand on his stomach, just needing the connection. I stared through the gap in the curtains, catching sight of the street light's peach glow, where it highlighted the autumnal, burnt-orange leaves of a tree. Rain must have fallen. Droplets of it decorated the windowpane, some losing anchor then dribbling down in an erratic, zig-zag path. It reminded me of us, of how we'd been fine, safe and secure, then I'd fled from New York to try to hide from my omissions and it had sent us scuttling downwards, our path jerking left to right until we'd reached the next destination.

*This* was our next destination, back together after a time of intense uncertainty. We would have to talk eventually, clear the air, and although I felt we were in a perfect idyll right now, I was wise enough to know that it was only temporary.

We had to sort through the rubbish and discard what no longer mattered. Find our scattered emotions and put them back where they belonged. Gather the threads that had loosened and knit them back together.

I hoped it would be easy, that if we attacked the task side by side, we'd get it done in half the time. No one enjoyed doing a spring clean, but I felt that in order for us to move on without resentment lingering, we needed to grab our polish and bleach and scrub all the untidiness into non-existence.

I just had to hope Blake felt the same way.

# 3

In the darkness, we continued to rest in one another's arms—and I was glad it *was* dark, unless the weak light from the street lamp counted. Yes, we had things to talk about, and him not being able to see my face meant I'd be more comfortable expressing myself. I didn't know how to bring the subject of the lies up without it seeming as though I wanted to start an argument, dredging up a past that could do with remaining buried. But if we didn't address things, we might not be able to move on.

"I'm sorry," I whispered.

*That's a good start, isn't it?* Dad always said a person who could apologise was a good 'un. Someone who could admit they'd made a mistake was one you wanted in your corner.

"Me too, Herman. We were stupid, right?"

"Hmm."

Yes, we'd been stupid, should have been honest and open from the start, but then, would we be together now if we'd done that? Things could have gone so differently. My main need had been to have someone love me for myself and not my celebrity status. I realised I'd gone a bit too far with that and had let pride rule me. And it *had* come before a fall, too.

Those old sayings were usually right.

"I think we got caught up in finding someone who wanted us for us and it clouded our judgement," I said. "But we know now, don't we, that we're with the right person."

"I'm right next to who I need to be with." He squeezed me tighter. "What about you?"

"Gosh, yes. I can't see myself being with anyone else." And I couldn't. Since meeting Blake, I hadn't contemplated life with another man.

"Then we're okay?" he asked.

"More than okay."

I listened to his heartbeat and our breathing. I thought about his time in hospital, and how I'd spent that month thinking I'd never see him again. And all the while his brother, Connor, the man I'd dubbed Ginger because of his alarming red hair, had kept the information of the accident from me.

*Little git...*

"How did you feel? In hospital, I mean?" I drew circles on his belly with my fingertip.

"Lonely. I had people come by, family and such, but I was still lonely. You know what they say—you can feel alone in a crowded room." He sighed. It was ragged and heavy. "I didn't have the one person with me that should have been. You. Every day I waited for you to walk through the door to my room, and every night I went to sleep dejected. I'm not telling you this to make you feel bad—you had no idea I was even injured—but at the time I entertained all sorts of things."

"Like what? Tell me." I opened my eyes and waited. Silver spots danced in front of me from where I'd had my eyes so tightly shut.

"That you wouldn't want to be with me if I couldn't walk again. And that was one of the major worries at first. I couldn't expect you to be with me then, not when I was half a man. And that's what it felt like I was. I couldn't feel my legs for about two days, and I honestly thought I'd end up in a wheelchair. I tell you, it's a frightening prospect. You don't realise how much you rely on your body until parts of it don't function as they did before."

I couldn't fathom the prospect of not having control over my whole body. I vowed that if he needed to talk about that in future, I'd be there for him.

"The wheelchair wouldn't have mattered," I said, meaning it.

"It would. In the end it would." He stroked my back. "And there might not have been any kids. You know, because…"

"I know. And that wouldn't matter either."

"You don't want kids?"

"Only with you, so if you couldn't…" I paused. "Then no. No kids."

"Oh, woman. I wish I'd met you years ago. There can't be many out there like you. Everyone I've met prior to you wanted diamonds, parties, clothes, shopping sprees. Yet you? A homebody is what you are deep down."

I smiled—he'd got me so right. "I am. Diamonds are just sparkly stones that sit around your neck and on your fingers or wrists. They make you feel pretty for a little while, but wear them for long enough and they become normal. And parties—I attend so many they end up being the same—different theme and location but the usual people, the usual antics. Clothes—what are they but covers for our bodies? I'd rather wear my trusty tracksuit off the local market than a Dior gown. As for shopping sprees…well, you get all hot and flustered, annoyed with the crowds, and end up arriving home exhausted with your feet on fire. What's great about that?"

He laughed, his chest bobbing my head up and down.

"Seriously, though." I snuggled closer. "Did you really think I'd abandoned you?"

"Uh-huh. But you can understand why, right? I thought we had this amazing thing going, this instant connection, and although you went back to London, I really had it in my head we'd get together again someday. Then the accident happened. Connor…"

"Connor what?" I lifted my head to try to see his face but it was too dark.

"He said the scaffolding was secure, that he'd checked it after it had been put up. I didn't question why he did that—and maybe I should have because it isn't his job, he's my head accountant, shouldn't be concerning himself with site work—and during the nights in hospital, when I couldn't sleep and everything swirled round in my mind, I thought things I shouldn't have."

"What things?" I laid my head back down and held my breath, thinking I knew. I was thinking all manner of stuff myself regarding that orange-haired little man.

Roo-Roo, my best friend, had put the idea in my head earlier in the day that Ginger had held back the hospital information on purpose. I'd told Roo-Roo that Ginger seemed to care about Blake so that couldn't possibly be true. But this scaffolding thing brought new, sinister thoughts about Ginger, ones I wasn't sure about. Were they my usual imaginings, or were they real? My gut instinct said that Ginger was a bad egg, but how could I know for sure—because I didn't know him at all, not really.

Ginger and Blake had some kind of problem standing between them, I'd sensed that when I'd first met Ginger, but did Blake really think Ginger had…? No, surely his brother wouldn't do that.

*Off in Daydream Land again, missus, thinking you're on a police case or something? I'll be flashing an imaginary detective badge in a second and demanding to see more evidence. Good grief!*

I prompted him again. "What things?"

"I thought maybe…that maybe he'd loosened one of the clamps." Blake went rigid, as though waiting for my answer, thinking it would be negative, that I'd be horrified. "Forget I said that. It was probably the pain meds talking at the time. I'm ashamed of myself, and you're the first person I've told. I don't think I'll ever tell anyone else."

"No. There must have been a reason for you to think that way. That kind of thing doesn't just come out of the blue. Like you said, why would he even be checking it?"

He laughed wryly. "That's where another bad thought comes in. I convinced myself he'd been seen on the construction site so that's why he said he'd checked the scaff. At one point, I was so high on morphine that I asked him about it. He denied it, looked so sincere that I hated myself. I haven't spoken to him about it since."

"So not only were you thinking stuff like that, I wasn't there either, to help you through it." I felt awful, even though it wasn't my fault. "All that time I'd been going through my own kind of hell, thinking you were prepared to let what we had go, that you wouldn't come to me, yet I didn't know you were injured. And I don't mean to sound nasty against your brother, but he didn't tell me, didn't pass on your message that you'd had a fall, and I think he *did* do that on purpose. I'd have been on a plane like a shot if I'd known."

"I asked him every day if he'd sent another email, just in case you hadn't gotten the last, and he even went so far as to say he'd called you and left a message on your answer phone."

I sucked in a breath. *The liar!* "I don't have an answer phone at home. Unless he meant my mobile, and I didn't get any kind of message from him at all."

Ginger was such a pig! I wondered what was it between them that made Ginger act the way he did with Blake. I didn't know much about their childhood yet, but I aimed to find out. There were issues there that needed sorting out. Maybe I could help with that. I wasn't exactly a relationship expert, but if they wanted to talk with me as middle man, I was willing to give it a go.

Although I'd never forgive Ginger for keeping me in the dark about Blake's accident. How did he sleep at night?

"I'm so glad you're okay," I whispered.

A change of subject was needed. Digging up old bones wasn't going to make for a very pretty skeleton. Even though Blake had confessed to thinking bad things about his brother, I knew from how I felt about my sister, Jenna, that it was okay for me to say stuff about her, but if anyone else did, I'd want to rip their head off. If I pushed too far and spoke out of turn about Ginger, we might end up in yet another row.

"Me too." He sighed again. "For a while back there…"

I heard him swallow and realised this might be something he could only talk about in small doses.

"If you don't want to discuss it, I understand." I circled his belly button again, the hairs tickling my fingertip.

"It's difficult."

"I know."

A few minutes drifted by. I wondered where we'd go from here. We were together, that much was obvious, and we loved each other to distraction, but there was still so much to sort out. A little voice inside me said to leave things be, to let our relationship trickle along at its own pace, and I approved of that to a degree. I was all for having some lightness in my life. Carefree times where we just enjoyed our days. Where we smiled and laughed a lot. But I tended to want to know what my future held so I could plan things better. A louder, more insistent voice wanted to know whether we'd be moving in together at some point, and if we did, where we'd live.

This was a big thing to tackle so early on in our relationship, something I'd only ever entertained in my daydreams, and of course, in those it all went my way, exactly how I wanted it, a lovely little house in the suburbs of London, me and my dream man happy as Larry with our white-picket fence, two-point-four children and a dog with an ever-wagging tail and lolling tongue.

Reality never worked out that way, though. Relationships were give and take.

*I have to learn to be more elastic. This being together lark is all a bit harder than I thought. No wonder so many people split up. Relationships are a lot of work.*

"If I go all selfish on you, will you tell me?" I asked, determined to stop being so introspective and stop internally questioning every little thing.

He laughed, the sound rumbling in his chest. "Where did that come from?"

"Oh, I don't know. Just thinking."

"Yeah, I'll tell you, but I can bet in the future you might not remember you asked me to do that and end up chewing me out anyway."

It was my turn to laugh. "I might do." I paused, then, "I don't want to sound stalkerish, getting in too deep, too quick, but we've already established what we have isn't your average connection, and…" I hesitated to bare my soul in case I sounded…too needy—again.

*Argh at myself!*

"Go on…"

"I was scared a bit when we were apart." Okay, admitting things wasn't so painful after all. "I didn't know what to do with myself, like I'd lost a part of me. As though I'd left it behind in America." *Oh dear, did that sound loopy or what?* I decided to push on anyway. "And so now you're here, I feel as though I need answers. Something solid that I can remind myself of if we ever get into a spat again or have a misunderstanding. I hope that makes sense."

He pulled me closer, held me tight. "If you want to know where you stand, you stand right here with me. You're my woman, my everything. I can't promise that in the future I won't let you walk away if we row, but believe me, it'll only be for a cool-down period. I'll hunt you down and find you, and only when you tell me you don't want me will I back off. Is that assurance enough? It didn't sound too caveman, did it?"

"It sounded perfect." I kissed the top of his arm. "Cavemannish, stalkerish, and absolutely perfect. Do you want me to do the same?"

"Only if that's what you're prepared to do."

"I am. Walking away to cool down sounds good—so long as we both know that's the case. No more going through what we just did, when we weren't sure what the other wanted."

"Agreed."

"And coming to find *you* sounds even better." I closed my eyes and pictured myself madly running through fire and jumping over boulders that crashed in my path, shoving them out of the way with my bare hands so I could reach him, Supergirl style. Okay, a little dramatic, but that was how I felt. The term 'walking over hot coals'—I understood it now.

"Why's that?" He stroked my back, soft and light, easing out the kinks.

"Well, you've only got to think about it, haven't you? Let's go with an airport. You getting off a plane and me running towards you, all slow motion, my hair flying, me shouting out your name. It's romantic and lovely." I waited for him to answer. "Or maybe not."

He chuckled. "Yeah, I could go with that, although I'd rather be the one stalking, rescuing you off the top of a cliff on a stormy night, flinging you up on my horse and galloping off to a little hut where we spend the night on a rug in front of the fire."

"Hmm, now there's a beautiful thought. And you're getting into the romance thing. I'm liking that." I was actually *loving* it. How many men on the planet indulged their woman with what they thought of as soppy stuff? "So, this horse. Be careful how you answer now. What colour is it?"

"White."

"Yes!"

"What?"

I lifted my head and looked at him. A shaft of light from a street lamp crept through the curtains, giving his eyes an amber twinkle.

"That was the correct answer," I said. "A knight on a white horse, see? I knew we were made for each other."

"So did I." He played with a strand of my hair, wrapping it around one finger. His face showed how bemused he was and that he was indulging me. "Knew it from the second I met you."

A lump of emotion expanded in my throat.

"I'd hate for you to leave me, Herman," he said.

"I'd hate to leave you."
"Then don't. Stay in my arms forever."
"Forever is a long, long time."
"Good."

**Diary**

**No Words**

He's here! On my English townhouse doorstep! I am on cloud nine!

Thousands of miles, a whole ocean, and the chaos that is Heathrow airport no longer separates us. There are no words for this feeling I'm experiencing right at this moment in time. Bliss doesn't even come close.

He does love me. He can't get enough of me. I feel invincible. Like I can take on the world! Charlotte meets The Incredible Hulk but less angry and more ecstatic. How did I ever function without this person? Eeeeeek, I can't contain myself.

Cutting this short as I have to get back to my man ASAP!

☺ ←Picture this face with teeth showing—I haven't got time to draw them. TTFN!

# 4

**Diary**

**Time Flies When You're Having Fun!**

I can hardly believe a year has gone by since I met Blake. How quick was that? My goodness. We're off to Gianni's restaurant in a bit to celebrate our first anniversary together. Yes, here again in the good old U S of A – I've lost count of the times I've flown back and forth over the pond. And to think when I first came here I was unknown in this part of the world. And what about my career zooming off at super speed? The American public have taken to me so well that recently I've been in a tailspin. I've worked so hard promoting my singles and first album that New York has been my base, although really, what with me jetting all over the States, base isn't exactly the right word. More like somewhere to rest my head between locations. I've lived out of hotels for what seems like forever, but now it's time to bring some other things to the table. Like launching my own perfume and appearing on American TV shows.

Whoo hoo! ☺

David – thank goodness for having him as my manager – has told me that I have a couple of things I need to return to the UK for, then I'll be back here to work again. It's been so exciting, such a mad rush dashing from one job to the next and meeting new fans. He says I'm a real star now, a big one, known globally, and it's weird, but I still see myself as ordinary Charlotte Taylor.

Pinch myself moment!

Right, I must get along now. I have to get dressed. Tonight is the first time in ages that I've been able to spend longer than a few hours with Blake, so I'm determined to enjoy it, to relax before my crazy, brilliant life whisks me off in other directions! Long may it continue – yay!

Whee! ☺

We sat in the reception area of Gianni's at a small table near the snazzy bar, our chairs close so our thighs touched. I finished my cocktail – I'd be tipsy before I knew it. While Blake went and ordered us another round of drinks – we weren't due to eat until about eight so we had twenty minutes to kill – I let my mind wander back over the past few months. We'd become so in tune, and I liked to think I'd grown up a lot. Oh, I still had my insecure moments, but for the most part I reckoned I'd got my wayward emotions in check.

Time would continue to tell – who knew what the future might bring?

There had been no time to discuss where we'd live permanently – zipping around all over the place had meant I hadn't really thought too much about it. But tonight, with the realisation that wow, we'd been together a year, and being able to actually think properly this evening, the subject had popped into my mind.

Hmm. Maybe it was a discussion for another night, when we weren't in public.

A bark of ribald laughter had me turning to look towards the entrance.

*Oh no, is that…Ginger?*

I hadn't seen him in a long while—not since before Blake had turned up at my house last year and told me he couldn't live without me. And I was glad to have avoided the tangerine-haired man. Using work commitments as an excuse not to see him had been handy, but I didn't think I'd get away with not talking to him now.

*Here's hoping it's only a brief conversation, then…*

Blake returned to our table with the drinks, and Ginger laughed loudly again, drawing Blake's attention. Since getting out of hospital, Blake had met up with Ginger many times, and as far as I knew, everything was okay between them. I, however, still hadn't forgiven Ginger for lying about contacting me when Blake had fallen off the scaffolding, and my brain, when I'd had idle moments between jobs, had still insisted there had been more to that accident than met the eye.

I didn't think I'd ever shake the feeling that Ginger was up to no good—or at the very least, that he wasn't a very nice person.

Ginger spotted us and sailed over, suit jacket flapping, exposing a white shirt and a dark green tie that seemed to have a blob of hairy pink marshmallow attached to it.

"Well, fancy seeing you here," Ginger said to Blake, completely ignoring my existence.

*That's okay. I can return the favour if he wants it that way... And is it me, or did Ginger sound sarcastic then?*

Blake shook his hand. "Connor." He nodded curtly, as if to let his brother know he should make himself scarce.

"And, Charlotte, how lov... Hello," Ginger said.

He smiled at me with lips so tight I had an idea they'd crack. I almost dug into my bag for some cherry-flavoured balm for him.

"Hello, Connor," I said, pleased with myself for not calling him Ginger. "How are you?"

"Not too bad," he said, dragging a stool over from another table then plonking down on it at ours. "Mine's a beer." He winked at Blake.

"The bar's over there." Blake stared at him, saying something with his eyes that I couldn't quite read.

*Bugger off, bro?*

"So, you here for a meal?" Ginger ignored his brother and reached out to take a sip of Blake's drink.

*Oh wow, so rude...*

"You know we are." Blake took his drink away. "I told you why earlier."

Ginger slapped his forehead, an overly dramatic gesture. "Oh yes, your anniversary meal. How could I have forgotten that?" He smiled an apology—fake, if I was any judge. "Then again, seeing as I haven't clapped eyes on you, Charlotte, unless it's on TV or posters or whatever, it isn't surprising I kind of forgot you're dating my brother." He laughed. "I mean, it's not like you're actually together much, is it?"

"We're together enough," Blake snapped. "And how often we see each other isn't any of your concern."

"Touchy…" Ginger shoved his stool back then stood. "And there was me about to ask if you'd mind me joining you, but I suppose—"

"Not tonight." Blake drained his drink then rose. "Excuse me for a second," he said to me then turned away and headed towards a friend of his at the bar.

*Oh. Great.*

Visions of me accusing Ginger of trying to kill Blake swam through my mind, but instead of doing just that, I plastered on a smile. People recognised me in America now—this wasn't the time or place to show myself up. Already this evening, several people had approached me for autographs, which I'd gladly signed.

Ginger sat back down then propped his elbow on the table and leant towards me. "You know you're not even meant to be with him at all, right?"

I widened my eyes before I could stop myself. "Pardon?"

*Keep smiling. Don't let him see he's got to you.*

He grinned back. "Let's just say me not telling you he'd had an accident was for a reason."

*I knew there was something off about him. Why, the little…*

"I see," I said, determined to keep my cool. "But you omitting that information didn't work, did it. We got together anyway."

"But you're not right for him." Ginger cocked his head and stared at me a bit too hard for my liking.

"In your opinion." I kept my voice light.

"Which counts for a lot with Blake." He smirked then eased away from me. "I mean, it would only take a few words from me and you'd be cast aside." He flapped his hand as though I was nothing but an annoyance.

*You have no idea what he thinks you did...* "Is that right?"

"Yes, that's right. And really, you being together for a year... It's not really a year if you think about it. You haven't seen each other much—only for about two months of that year, if you add all the days and hours up. So he still doesn't know you too well."

"He knows enough—knows all he needs to." I wasn't about to say that Blake knew enough to be sure that we belonged together regardless of how often we saw each other. It was none of Ginger's business, and the less information he had, the better.

"Hmm." He flared his nostrils.

*What's that supposed to mean?* I was dying to ask him to elaborate, but at the same time I wanted him to just get up and walk out. To go away and leave us to it. Somehow, though, I knew that wasn't on his to-do list. He seemed the type who enjoyed causing trouble.

"You know"—he leant towards me again, covering his lips with the side of one finger—"I really think you ought to finish with him. You're not going to last the distance anyway, so you may as well end it now, before he gets too attached."

"We're already attached." I would love to have said 'at the hip' but sadly that wasn't the case—our workloads saw to that. "Look, I don't know what your problem is with me, but can't we resolve it? I'm going to be with Blake for a very long time, so we may as well at least try to get along."

"Ha!"

His outburst startled me, and I jumped a little, cursing myself for showing that he made me uneasy.

"My problem, little lady, is that I don't trust you. You're not in my future plans. You need to go away."

The manner in which he'd said that had my stomach churning. I'd taken it with sinister undertones, so I quickly recapped what he'd said to make sure I'd heard him right. The look on his face confirmed my suspicions—he really *didn't* want me in Blake's life.

*Why not?*

I asked him outright, quietly, still with a smile on my face.

"Because," he said, "although you appear a total airhead, I think you're actually quite clever and would know—"

*Know what?* I frowned. And what had me being clever got to do with anything? Was he trying to tell me he knew that I was aware he wasn't a good man? That I'd seen him for who he really was?

I noticed Blake had finished talking with his friend and that he was turning from the bar to come back to our table.

"Just watch out," Ginger whispered. "I'll be keeping my eye on you. One wrong move..."

A shiver went down my spine, but Blake appeared beside us quicker than I'd expected. Ginger stared at me as though warning me to keep my mouth shut, and really, what would I tell Blake anyway? That his brother had threatened me?

I excused myself and made my way to the ladies, mind spinning with scenarios. I was confused as to what Ginger had actually meant—and whether he'd even been acting weirdly or if my overactive imagination had just made it seem that way. The scaffolding incident came to mind, and after the conversation I'd just had, and witnessing the look in Ginger's eyes, I could well see him sabotaging that construction site.

It was too vast to fully take in. Never in my life had I thought I'd *really* contemplate this kind of thing. Yes, I'd thought about it when Blake had told me his suspicions, but honestly…

No, this was just crazy. I'd been surviving on little sleep and had taken my chat with Ginger completely the wrong way. But as I finished up in the bathroom, an insistent voice told me I hadn't.

I returned to the reception area and directed my gaze at our table immediately. Ginger was gone—*thank goodness for that!*—and Blake sat there in a daze with a frown firmly in place, sipping his drink. Had Ginger said something to him too?

I sat, gave Blake a wide smile, then had a sip of my drink, pleased my hand wasn't shaking. "Everything okay?"

"Yeah." Blake shook himself out of his trance. "Why wouldn't it be? I'm with the most wonderful woman on the planet."

I rested a hand on one of his. "It's just that you look troubled."

He shook his head. "It's nothing. Just seeing Connor here annoyed me. I told him I'd booked a table and why, and it pissed me off that he turned up anyway. Like he *wanted* to interrupt. I just don't understand him."

"Has he gone up to eat?" I glanced at the stairs that led to the upper dining room.

"No, that's just the thing. You went to the restroom then he said goodbye and left." He sighed, as though trying to work his brother out. "I don't get him at all. Why would he want to turn up like that then just go?"

I wasn't about to voice the fact that I thought Ginger's sole purpose had been to give me his bizarre message. This was our anniversary, and I didn't want it spoiled any further. "Look, maybe he thought he could join us or something, make it a bigger celebration. Or maybe he was just passing, remembered we were here, and dropped in to say hi."

I hated defending the little dweeb, but it was better than ruining our night.

"Hmm. You're probably right." He lowered his stiff shoulders then smiled. "Come on, drink up. We have something to celebrate."

I laughed, looking forward to tumbling into bed and getting a proper night's sleep, which would take my worries about Ginger away. The rest would relax me, then tomorrow we'd wake up and pack, ready to board our flight to London. Blake had taken some time off to accompany me this time, and although I'd be working, it would be great for him to come along and see the kind of things I did every day.

As we took the stairs to the restaurant, I knew Ginger's appearance would still taint the evening—and beyond. For now, though, I shoved him to the back of my mind and promised myself that when I had more time, I'd go through what he'd said and see if I could make better sense of it.

*Time. What's that again?*

I grinned, pleased that I was so busy. After all, my life was everything I'd dreamed of and more.

# 5

Tonight we were back in the UK, going to a film premiere, some horror flick that I wouldn't usually want to see. David had said The Snorters, aka some models that I knew, had sent me two tickets to the event. He'd suggested I go to the premiere and take it as an opportunity to do some networking. Oh my word, how could I have said no when it would give me a chance to cosy up to Blake in the semi-darkness? I was all for snuggling next to him, and besides, watching gritty thrillers in The Big Apple had kind of helped me see that even though a film might be scary, it wasn't *that* bad to watch.

Via David, I'd also got wind of who one of the main actresses was. I hadn't been able to believe my ears when I'd heard. Who knew Deborah Cressida—aka Bitcherella, a mean woman from my early days—had been working on a film set all this time and had kept it below the radar? Wow. Normally, she couldn't keep anything quiet and loved to blurt everyone's business, but it seemed she wanted to keep her own life close to her chest. That figured! Apparently, The Snorters were also playing cameo parts, and David had said the whole cast had basically been sworn to secrecy throughout filming. He'd put it to me that because I'd done the runway job last year with The Snorters, it might be a good idea to show them my support.

So I was excited to be going, and of course, it was my first UK public outing with Blake. I was excited to show him off. Couldn't wait for all and sundry to see how happy I was since I'd found him. My belly did somersaults and a million back flips every time I thought about arriving outside the cinema, getting out of the car—then the big reveal.

*Look, people, look at my glorious, sexy man!*

I smiled at myself in the bathroom mirror. One of those big cheesy grins that made my eyes twinkle. I was *so* happy—I couldn't begin to express how much. I mean, I thought I'd lost Blake, and now, here we were, getting ready to go out.

*SQUEAL!*

"Will you be long?" Blake asked, yanking me out of perusing-my-face-for-blemishes mode.

I opened the bathroom door to find him standing there in the buff. *Whoa.* He was *here,* with *me,* with *no clothes on*. Oh my goodness, the amount of times I could have pinched myself lately. By rights I should be covered in bruises.

"Just checking my eyebrows," I said, conscious that I'd had them waxed and plucked that morning and I wanted to make sure I didn't resemble one of The Snorters—arrow eyebrows weren't my cup of tea.

"They're fine," he said and walked into the en suite. "They're like…eyebrows."

God bless him, but he just didn't get womanly foibles.

"Oh, they're not *just* eyebrows." I moved my face closer to the mirror to get a better look. "They're potentially newsworthy. Some of the magazines pick up on the smallest things and make a big deal about them."

"You live in a strange world, Herman, but I kinda know what you mean."

I watched the reflection of Blake switching on the shower behind me. Talk about a great chance to nose at him while he wasn't aware of it. Lordy, I'd never get over how lucky I was. My man had a body to die for—all those muscles were enough to send a girl doolally.

"And you don't?" I asked, not needing to refer to how Blake regularly felt he had to hide from the press. I wondered how he'd cope with tonight. "Will you be okay?" I turned to face him as he stepped into the shower cubicle. "I mean, being in the limelight later?"

He stood under the spray and tipped his head back. While he shampooed his hair, he closed his eyes and smiled. "I'll be fine. There's a difference in having my photo taken when I know it's being taken compared to the press invading my privacy and just snapping them." He smoothed his hands over his hair to get the bubbles out.

"Hmm, I'm with you."

I knew exactly what he meant. I felt the same.

I left him to it and walked into the bedroom feeling as light as a feather. I stripped off my towel then shrugged into my dressing gown. Rupert, or Roo-Roo as I called him, had agreed to nip round to do my makeup and he'd be here soon.

Right on cue, the doorbell chimed. I rushed down the stairs as though flying, reaching the front door out of breath and feeling giddy. The good kind of giddy, where everything was all right in my world. I checked through the peephole and, seeing Roo-Roo on the other side, his face skewed by the little spyhole, I swung the door open.

"Oh my." He looked me up and down. "Someone appears to be well-loved." He stepped inside, closed the door behind him, then followed me into the small room off my kitchen that I liked to think of as my personal salon.

"I am." I beamed at him—a smile brighter than a Porsche's headlights, I reckoned—and sat in my comfy leather hairdressing chair. "And you need to leave by the side door when you're finished, remember that, so there's no chance of you spotting Blake."

Roo-Roo sighed dramatically—as always—and waved his hand midair. "Yes, reduced to the tradesman's entrance, I know. And how could I forget? You went on and on about me not seeing Blake until later because you wanted me to see him at the same time as everyone else." He delved about in my makeup drawer. "Did you get those new false eyelashes I told you about? Ah, yes, here they are. Very good, petal. Glad you took notice of something I said."

I swatted his arm. "Hey, it's not every day a girl finds her dream man on her doorstep when she'd thought she'd never see him again. And it's not every day a woman's career explodes overseas. We've been…busy lately, but I did get a second to order the lashes online."

"Hmm." Rupert started applying my foundation. "Busy indeed. Care to share?"

"Erm…quite frankly, no. Some things have to remain private. Best friend or not, there are some titbits you don't need to know."

He laughed, then we settled into our usual routine. I sat still and quiet, and he hummed some tune or other. It wouldn't be long before he'd want to blurt the latest gossip and, true to form, once he was at the lipstick stage, he gave his usual grunt.

I waited for what he was about to say, although I knew what was coming.

"So," he said, drawing out the 'O', "what about Bitcherella, then?"

"Oh, I know!" I thought about how Deborah must be feeling tonight. "Look, I know she's not a particularly nice person, but I can't help feeling for her about this evening. She'll be so nervous, what with it being her film debut."

"Nervous? Her?" Rupert made a rude sound. "Not on your life, missus. She'll be loving all the attention. And of course, she'll be the best actress that ever lived—and no one had better tell her otherwise." He touched up my eyeshadow. "And do you know what? She'll be crap. I'll bet you one hundred pounds she's awful."

I wasn't so sure. "I happen to think she'll be quite good."

"So we have a bet?" Rupert cocked his head and studied my face.

"Okay." I hoped I'd win it. Much as Deborah was horrible to people, for some odd reason I wanted to believe that somewhere deep inside her was a nice person waiting to come out.

"Right, we're done." Rupert smiled. "And you look absolutely gorge, my dear. Now, I really must use your toilet..."

"Uh, no you don't." I stood then moved over to the door that led into the rest of the house to stop him leaving the room. "I know what you're like. You'll just happen to swan into my bathroom and introduce yourself to Blake. Off out with you." I swished my hand to indicate the side door. "I'm sure you can hold it until you get home."

"Oh, I'm wounded!" He did one of his dramatic poses, all back of the hand against his brow, his eyes narrowed in supposed pain. "But you got me. That's exactly what I was going to do. It's weird that you've been with him so long yet I haven't met him yet. Yes, yes, *you've been busy*. So, now my perfect plan has been foiled, I shall leave you to it and see you later." He air-kissed my cheeks then flounced to the 'tradesman's exit'. "See you later, tater!"

As I locked up, I laughed to myself about how Rupert never failed to make things so much brighter. I hoped he'd get along with Blake. And, more importantly, I hoped he didn't come across as super-protective like he had with everyone else. Roo-Roo was a darling, and my best friend besides Blake and Jenna, but he had a tendency to be a bit feisty when it came to looking after me.

And argh, I'd forgotten to tell him about that weird episode with Ginger at Gianni's. Roo-Roo would know exactly what that man was playing at. I'd have to talk to him about it some other time when I got a spare moment.

I glanced at the clock and realised I shouldn't have locked the side door. Chantelle, my lovely hairdresser, would be here any second. The sound of a car engine rumbled, and I peeked out of the window to see if it was her. Yes, there she was, parking up in front of the house. I opened the door, let her in, and so the hair-do shenanigans began.

Once she was done and had left, I returned to my bedroom. Blake was on the bed watching TV. I stalled in the doorway, taking in the sight of him.

He glanced from the TV to me, widened his eyes then sat up quickly. "Wow, look at you."

Blake hadn't seen me this dressed up before—unless you counted the pictures of me he'd seen on my laptop or on TV and posters. Yeah, I'd got dolled up when we'd been out in New York, but this was Celebland hair and makeup. Next, I'd be putting on a Celebland dress, a red little number with sparkles in the material that made me feel pretty and comfortable with how I looked.

I smiled at him, feeling like me but knowing, from his facial expression, I didn't look like me.

"Where's my Herman gone?" he asked.

"Oh, she's still here." I walked over to my wardrobe to take out the cute dress. "She's just hiding under makeup, that's all." I slid my dressing gown off then stepped into the dress, pulling it up my body. "Would you mind zipping me up?"

"Mind? Hell, no, woman!"

Blake leapt off the bed, coming towards me at top speed. I held my breath. He stood behind me, his body heat warming my back.

"You're just so adorable," he breathed, slowly raising my zip. "And in a few short hours that zip's going to be coming right back down." He kissed my exposed shoulder. "And this dress? It's going to be forgotten on the floor."

I shivered with the images he was creating in my mind and knew if I didn't move away from him I'd turn and press myself against him. I let out the breath I'd held. "That's something to look forward to."

"Absolutely right it is." He smoothed his hands up and down my arms, and the scent of him wafted all around me.

I resisted the urge to swivel around. "But you need to get your suit on. We have to be there in just under an hour." I could do with not going now, but showing Blake off was so exciting and something I'd really been longing to do.

"Spoilsport."

He left me then, moving to the wardrobe, where he pulled out one of his suits and a crisp white shirt. I bent to pick up my red sling-back shoes then went down to the living room. I checked through my little ruby-encrusted clutch—fake stones that glittered as the light caught them—to make sure I had my keys, lipstick and phone. Then I stared through the window, waiting for the car to arrive. Waiting for Blake to come down and take my breath away at the sight of him.

It seemed as though I stood there for ages.

And now there he was, all spruced up and ready to go in a black suit, white shirt and a red tie. I smiled at that—his tie matching my dress—and I didn't care if someone made a comment about our colour-coded clothes. It touched me that he'd thought to make the effort.

Before I could rush forward, grip his lapels and kiss him stupid, headlights blazed through the window. "You look…" I swallowed. "Lovely."

Blake winked. "Our carriage awaits, m'lady." He smiled. "Did that sound English then or did I fail at the London accent?"

"You failed, but I love you anyway." I laughed and slid on my shoes, hoping to goodness they didn't have a mind to pinch my toes as the evening wore on.

"Good job I don't get offended easily," he said as we left the house.

In the back of the car, I made sure my dress wasn't going to get too crumpled then leant against Blake. Nerves decided to kick in. It wasn't even a movie that had anything to do with me, but still, there was the red carpet to walk down once we got there and pictures to be taken.

He reached across to hold my hand, and immediately the nerves didn't ping around so much. Blake had the wonderful ability to calm me.

I didn't want it any other way. Ever.

# 6

The driver dropped us off outside the theatre. Blake and I waited by the kerb for our turn to go inside, receiving curious stares from some of the crowd. I linked my arm with Blake's and squeezed, smiling my head off as he looked down at me with a massive smile of his own. This was so wonderful, standing beside him instead of David—or as was sometimes the case, by myself. I felt all protected, like nothing bad could ever happen as long as Blake was next to me.

Oh, yeah, I'd found my soulmate all right.

I didn't want to take my eyes off him and could have stood there and gazed up at him all night, but a familiar shriek of laughter pulled my attention from him. I glanced around and saw that Deborah had arrived, and as she moved away from her car, she milked the limelight. Cameras flashed and photographers shouted her name. She was in her element, and I knew how she must be feeling. This was her turn to shine in her own right—as a film star, not just some woman who hung around celebrities, snooping for juicy stories to sell. Maybe she'd stop doing that now she'd found her place in the sparkly world she so enjoyed being a part of.

She had on a pretty teal sheath dress that clung to her toned body. The material looked heavy. Around her shoulders she wore a fluffy cream stole, her long hair a splash of black against it. And oh, a beautiful diamond necklace twinkled, one I was sure would have cost a fortune. A pair of matching teal shoes finished her outfit off nicely, and she walked in them without a trace of fear that she might trip over.

If only I could be so elegant!

"That's Deborah Cressida," I whispered to Blake. I'd told him about her—how she made me feel sometimes, and how she'd bluntly expressed the fact that she didn't like me, even though I'd done nothing to warrant her hate.

"Lovely," Blake said, the word full of sarcasm.

He didn't let his attention linger on her for more than a second or two. She was a beauty, no doubt about it, and I'd always thought any man who looked at her couldn't help but fall in love just a little bit.

"I wonder what role she's playing?" I said quietly, intrigued to see how she fared at acting. I wanted to win my bet with Rupert so badly.

Going by Deborah's performances at parties, I'd convinced myself she'd do a *very* good job. She knew how to give that smouldering look that could bring a man to his knees.

"Who cares?" Blake shrugged. "She's just another pretty face in the crowd, you know? You, on the other hand…"

People like Deborah always seemed to get whatever person they set their sights on. I hoped to goodness she wouldn't set her sights on Blake once she clapped eyes on him. That could make for some awkward moments.

"Me on the other hand what?" I was still staring at Deborah, mesmerised by her sparkling smile and the ease with which she fitted so well under the spotlight.

"You stand out from that crowd."

That made me feel heaps better. I squeezed his arm again.

Another car drew up behind us, and we moved out of the way so the occupants had space to get out. I turned to see The Snorters, dressed in matching pink dresses and impossibly high-heeled shoes, elegantly climbing out of a white limousine. Before I knew it, they'd bumped into the back of us, jostling me away from Blake. I sidled along to where I thought Blake was. It was so crowded with stars and photographers that I couldn't see his face but I was relieved when, in my peripheral vision, I saw the sleeve of his suit.

Deborah lingered on the red carpet, lifting her hand and widening her eyes as yet another car came to a stop at the kerb. She smiled hard at whoever got out and waved them over, a huge emerald ring engulfing one of her fingers. I caught sight of a startling white suit with multi-coloured rhinestones on the shoulders of the jacket. Then I spotted a sleek, dark head, a wide boxer's neck, and huge sunglasses, even though it was night-time.

*Oh bugger.* It was Twenny Pee, *the* rapper of the year, and a man I'd dabbled with just before I'd met Blake. I had been tipsy and lonely, desperate for some form of closeness that friends and family just couldn't provide. And I'd wanted to fit in with the others in Celebland—my word, how I'd wanted to fit in.

Somehow, Deborah had found out about the dalliance and had spent no time in letting me know she was aware. She'd given me a twenty pence piece, and now I kind of knew how she'd got such information on me. It seemed she and Twenny were good friends these days, something I'd never thought would happen because he'd disliked her not so long ago. Some people were so fickle.

Oh well, there was no time to ponder on that now. I'd told Blake about my past, and to be honest, I didn't think he felt threatened that I'd been involved with Twenny.

Deborah clutched onto Twenny's arm, grinning for some headline-hungry poses, and I wondered if they were an actual item or if he'd just agreed to pose with her to get the press talking. But if they were together-together, it made me wonder whether that was why she looked genuinely happy, and I related to that so much. I couldn't wait to pose myself, standing there with Blake so we could announce, just by us standing there together, that we were an official, honest-to-goodness couple.

The red-carpet manager called my name loudly and waved us over. Deborah rolled her eyes at that then pursed her lips as she was ushered inside the theatre out of sight. She obviously hadn't been done with strutting her stuff for the crowd. I grabbed Blake's hand and walked forward, tugging him along behind me. This was my moment to really show him off. I smiled for the cameras, glancing left then right as I always did, making sure everyone got whatever shots of me they wanted. Some fans screamed out, and I made a move to step forward and sign the CD cases they were flapping around, but Blake held me back. I didn't have time to turn to him and give him a questioning look, and it wouldn't have been a good idea anyway, not with the press all around us, waiting to catch any sign of discord they could.

So we climbed the three steps up to the theatre doors and I was pleased when Blake stood behind me. I drew his arm across my belly, but it felt as though he was resisting it being placed there. Maybe he was a little nervous at being in front of such a large crowd. Again, no time to mull it over. People were yelling my name, and others shouted, "Is this your new fella, Lola?" and "You finally found the love of your life?"

I nodded, smiling so hard my cheeks bunched into apples.

Yes! This was what I wanted, my man showing every other man out there that this lady was no longer up for grabs. *This* lady was well and truly in love—*and don't you forget it, folks!*—and she wanted the whole wide world to know it.

"Bloody hell," one of the photographers closest to us muttered. "Who'd have thought it?"

I took it to mean he was referring to Blake and that he must know of him being a successful businessman who had built stadiums, celebrity homes and all manner of great things in America. I was so proud of Blake I could burst!

A strangely hot blast of air hit my shoulder from behind. Either Blake was breathing super heavily to combat his nerves or some kind of heater had been switched on above the theatre doors. I turned to glance up at him, but to my horror, I stared into eyes that were set in an orange-coloured face and held teeth so large and white I could have squinted from the glare.

I was standing with none other than music mogul, Johnny Bravo.

*Oh. My. Giddy. Aunt.*

"Oh, shit!" I let slip out, mortified that he was the one who had his arm draped across my belly and his pelvis all but sewn to my backside. "What? How?"

I zipped my mind back to when I'd grabbed what I'd thought was Blake's hand. It had felt the same as his, was even the same size. But I hadn't actually looked to check it was him, instead so focused on climbing those steps and showing him off that this humongous, awful error had been made. And the press! They'd asked if this was my new fella and I'd bloody *nodded.*

"Where's Blake?" I whispered, keeping a smile on my face for the crowd.

"Who the hell is Blake, babe?" Johnny shouted.

Argh! How had I forgotten he always shouted instead of spoke?

"My boyfriend!" I said loudly, quickly adding, "Oh, you're such a scream! Hey, everyone, he thought it would be funny to pose as my boyfriend!" I joke-slapped his chest and moved my bum away from him then went on, "But my real boyfriend is..." I scanned the gathering at the bottom of the steps.

Blake was nowhere to be seen.

I frantically searched for him, spotting him a metre or so away being led inside the theatre by an usher.

"Oh, he's right there, look," I said and jerked my thumb in his direction, wishing I could just run away to be with him.

"So you're not with *him*?" someone called, referring to Johnny Bravo.

I turned back to the photographers, wanting to say, 'Bloody hell, no!' but instead I shook my head. My cheeks grew really hot, and it made me think of Roo-Roo telling me not to get flustered or my foundation would melt. So I took a deep breath to calm down then said, "He loves playing tricks, that one." I laughed, giving Johnny a cheeky grin—play-acting, that's all it was. I couldn't afford to offend him.

"Yeah, tricks and fun are what I'm all about," Johnny shouted. Titters and whoops from the crowd made him smile. "And, nice as it's been getting up to mischief, we have a film to watch. *Ciao* for now!"

He took my hand and led me inside, and I was so grateful for that. Steering us towards his girlfriend, Johnny laughed to himself, and I wondered if he'd engineered me grabbing his hand out there on purpose.

"Anjellika!" he bellowed out then homed in on his girlfriend, who stood beside Blake at the rear of the foyer. "Where did you get to, babe?"

I let go of Johnny's hand and would have flung myself into Blake's arms if people weren't watching us so closely. I twined my fingers with his to make sure I didn't lose him again. After Johnny and Anjellika had walked away, I went up on tiptoes to whisper in Blake's ear.

"Oh, I am *so sorry* about that." I was actually horrified about the whole scenario, more than a bit upset that I hadn't been able to show Blake off like I'd wanted to. He'd been excited about it too, and to know his enjoyment might have been dulled somewhat had me feeling even worse.

"You've got to admit, that was funny." Blake chuckled and cupped my cheek with one hand. "I saw you grab his hand and cart him off, but you zipped up those steps so fast I didn't have time to call out and let you know."

"They thought he was my *boyfriend.*" My face was flaming hot now and shivers roared up and down my back. "Oh, the thought of that just..."

"But you saved the situation beautifully." Blake rubbed his thumb across my cheek. "And there will be other times you can show me off. Come on now, don't tell me you can't see the funny side."

Oh, I could, and I was glad to. Feeling mortified all night would have spoiled the evening, and I wanted to enjoy it. "Hmm, I suppose..."

Before we could discuss it any further, Deborah coasted towards us like an elegant yacht, parting the milling celeb crowd in soft ripples. She had Twenny in tow, and my tummy rolled over as I anticipated her saying something mean.

"Oh, so lovely of you to come." She blatantly gave Blake her come-to-bed look.

I wanted to scratch her eyes out.

"Nice to be here." My pulse thudded hard in my neck as I struggled to bat away the influx of uneasiness barging through me. "And it's great to hear you're one of the cast. I'm really pleased for you."

She took that moment to glance away from Blake and give me a spiteful glare. "Oh, how…lovely of you to say that." She appeared confused for a second, as though she wasn't sure if I'd meant what I'd said. Then her usual resting bitch face came back, masking whatever emotions she was feeling. "And I see you've brought a man with you." She treated Blake to one of her beautiful smiles. "My, you go through them back to back, don't you, Lola?"

*Oh, that sounds awful. Like I'm a tart and I put it about.*

Blake smiled at me, making me feel a bit better.

"As you can see…" Deborah turned to gaze at Twenny, who stood behind her like some kind of doting lapdog, seemingly in a world of his own. "I'm with one of your cast-offs tonight."

"Great!" I didn't know what else to say. And what was she going to say next? Would she go into detail about my time with Twenny, seeing as he didn't appear to be listening? That would be totally embarrassing. And what if she had it in her head to steal Blake away from me? She'd done it to so many people in the past that it wouldn't surprise me.

I couldn't allow that to happen, couldn't even let her try.

"Anyway, I've had enough of this little chat. I get bored so easily…" She flashed her perfect teeth at Blake. "Goodbye." She reached up to lay a hand on his shoulder…and massaged it.

*What the…?*

"For now," she whispered then blew him a kiss.

I stared after her as she walked away, my cheeks hotter than they'd ever been in my life. Who did she think she was? Red mist filled my vision. I was all but ready to get into a cat fight if she thought she could mess around with my Blake.

His chuckle brought me out of my angry fog and I looked up at him.

"She's not my type, Herman," he said. "Not my type *at all.*"

# 7

**Diary**

**Only Me**

Eeerrrgggghhh! Deborah Cressida. She really is a Bitcherella! What is it with the constant silent threats and hints that she's going to spill the beans on every embarrassing moment in my life, completely driving Blake away? Or is that just my imagination, me worrying over nothing? What can she tell him anyway?

Let's see:

I slipped off a penis chair at a party. (Blake already knows.)

I used duct tape instead of proper boob tape to hold myself up at the award ceremony. (I'm almost sure I told him about that too at some point. Yeah, I did. And he laughed, saying I'd been inventive and it was nothing to be ashamed of. So there.)

I've slept with Twenny Pee. (He definitely knows about that. Okay, not all the gritty deets, but he's aware the rapper's from my past. And he isn't bothered. Or he doesn't seem to be. So why am I bothered?)

There's got to be something about *her* that's making me feel uneasy. Maybe it's because I know what she's like, what she gets up to. You know, telling tales on people, spreading gossip and whatever.

So let's think about this properly, once and for all. Okay. I know exactly what it is. I'm going to sound ridiculous, but it doesn't matter because this is just for my eyes only. Here goes.

Maybe she wants to take away my happiness because underneath it all, she's unhappy. Or… Oh, can I even bear to write it?

Right.

One. Two. Three. Go!

Maybe she wants Blake for herself!

There. I've said it. And it isn't implausible. She always was attracted to the green—she could have found out how much he's worth and wants all his cash! Anything that shines and glitters or speaks money and she's there.

Little magpie.

Well, she won't get my man, not now, not ever.

Note to self: Avoid that woman like the plague. She is bad news!

Still, something good came out of the evening. I finally introduced my beloved Roo-Roo to Blake and they got on like a house on fire. Whoo hoo! When Roo-Roo saw him, he squealed in his usual way and hugged the breath out of him. So funny! Blake hid his shock well—mind you, I'd warned him Roo-Roo was a hugger. Blake even cuddled him back! My life will be so complete once Dad and Jenna meet him too.

I *must* sort that out—sometimes I'm just far too busy, and they have asked why I haven't taken him over to see them. Oops!

Oh, and I won the bet. Deborah was brilliant in her acting role. I'll collect my hundred pounds from Rupert next time I see him. ☺ Winner!

Today I had a quick job to do. On our way to the recording studio, I stared out of the car window and thought about last night. Blake had assured me that I was all he'd ever need. It was as though he'd known exactly what to say and had read my thoughts about Deborah trying to snatch him away from me.

When he'd fallen asleep, I'd stayed awake for ages, writing my diary and thinking on how I must have trust issues or something. Or maybe I felt so worried about losing Blake that I was subconsciously looking for reasons that he might walk away. I really ought to stop doing that, especially because I'd woken up thinking about it too. If I wasn't careful, Deborah and her grabby little hands would take over my mind, infecting my life, and I'd be so wrapped up in fretting about her that I wouldn't enjoy my time with Blake.

And that just wouldn't do.

I switched my thoughts to the day ahead. I needed to go into the studio and listen to some of the tracks I had been working on for my second album, and make sure I was happy with them. Blake was by my side now, his thigh pressed to mine, and I was excited to be sharing this experience with him. It would give him another insight into what I did for a living. He'd said earlier that he was looking forward to it and that he found my life fascinating.

*Oh, happy days!*

As we drew up to a parking spot behind the studio building, I took the chance to give Blake a quick kiss while the driver got out to open one of the rear doors. It was on Blake's side, so he got out first and waited for me to join him. He took my hand, thanked the driver, then escorted me through the glass double doors and into the foyer.

"Ah, Lola," the receptionist said, a petite young woman with blonde pigtails and a sweet smile. "Go on up, they're ready for you."

"Thanks, Georgina." I smiled at her then led Blake to the lift.

Once inside, he took me in his arms and leant me backwards, supporting the top of my spine with one hand, his other around my waist. *Oh my, what a romantic!*

"You are the best thing to have ever happened to me, did you know that?" he asked in between kissing a rather delightful path up my neck.

"Mmm, you've told me often enough, but I'll never get tired of hearing it."

"I'll never stop saying it."

He pulled me upright, drawing me close, and I rested my cheek on his chest. I loved doing that, hearing his heartbeat.

Sadly, the lift dinged then it lurched to a stop. I eased away from him as the doors slid open, and we stepped out into a carpeted corridor that had rooms at either end.

I grasped his hand. "This way." I tugged him to the right, going through to a lounge, where artists usually sat on the sofas while waiting for their spot in the studio.

A few coffee cups littered a small table and, despite the smoking ban, an ashtray overflowed with butts. One of the latest music magazines had been left spread out on a sofa, and I spotted a close-up image of Twenny, flashing his gold grills, those big sunglasses of his covering most of his face. I glanced away to my left at a large internal window. Beyond it, one of the sound rooms was occupied by a tech and an up-and-coming artist, a young man whose voice didn't match his body. He was kind of weedy and looked about sixteen, but he was twenty-five and roared out lyrics like a bear.

"We're in the next one," I said and walked towards a second window.

Blake smiled. He stared around as though in wonder. "I never thought I'd be in a place like this. As a kid, you think about being a rock star, but to actually be here? Feels surreal."

"I know what you mean." And I did. I still couldn't get over the fact that this was my place of work—well, one of them anyway—and I'd often thought whether there'd ever come a time when it became absolutely normal and not a novelty.

I peered through the window. Aleks was there, the guy I worked with on sound and pitch, and he waved us in. I pushed the door open, glancing at Blake just to check he was okay and that he was right behind me. He smiled, and I was reassured.

"Hey, Aleks." I walked over to him and gave him a hug.

He returned it, as well as planting two air kisses either side of my head. "Great to see you, doll. You're looking mighty relaxed. All that work must do you the world of good."

I loved Aleks to bits and couldn't wait to introduce him to Blake. "It does, and I've brought along this wonderful man here..." I reached out to take Blake's hand and urged him closer. "Blake, this is Aleks—Aleks, Blake."

"Great to meet you at last, man." Aleks shook Blake's hand.

"Feeling's mutual." Blake nodded.

"Ah, a fellow American. Awesome!" Aleks drew Blake into a man-hug, slapping him on the back. "Where you from?"

"New York. You?"

"Brooklyn. Can't you tell?"

They laughed—it must have been some kind of US joke about accents or something—but whatever it was I didn't care. They were getting along and it made me so pleased because Blake wouldn't feel uncomfortable now.

Aleks stepped back then moved to his equipment. "Tracks are darn good, Lola. You ought to hear *Driving into the Light*. Man, it rocks. Kicks ass."

A swell of pride bubbled up inside me. I'd written that one completely by myself, so to know it had turned out great gave me a massive sense of personal achievement. Being here, where I'd always longed to be, growing up, with Blake a part of it—wow, I couldn't get any happier.

I sat at the mixing desk, beckoning Blake to come and join us. He shook his head, and I realised he was happy to stand against the wall, watching, taking it all in. Knowing he was comfortable, I concentrated on what Aleks was saying.

"So the only one I think we have a problem with is *Midnight Longing*." Aleks tapped the end of a pencil on the desk. "And that's nothing to do with your singing. It's the bridge. You know that part—"

"Where the backing track switches to really fast?" I nodded. "I know what you mean. It kind of gets in the way when I'm singing, if that makes sense. Like I'm waiting for it to come, knowing I have to change gears, and it puts me off."

"We could go with switching that up." Aleks stared through the window. "Oh, man. Between you and me, I'm dreading it when you've gone. I have that crazy piece of ass coming in. She wants to lay down a track. You can bet your bottom dollar she'll need the voice modifier on."

I turned to look over my shoulder, and my jaw, if it had been long enough, would have dropped right into my lap. Oh my God, Deborah Cressida stood on the other side of the glass wearing what I could only describe as a bright red corset with black lace ruffled up as a trim and…was that a feather contraption on her head?

A strangled sound came from Blake's direction. I snatched a peek at him, but he was staring intently towards the mixing desk and Aleks.

*Why does she have to be here, today of all days? Argh!*

Thank goodness this room was soundproof. Having her hearing my very personal songs before the public did wasn't something I wanted to happen.

"Like I said, man"—Aleks winked at Blake—"crazy piece of ass. Be glad you don't have to deal with her."

Blake cleared his throat. I gave Deborah my attention again—much to my annoyance, but I couldn't help myself. There she was, prancing about, giving the men some kind of dance that looked like she was an irate chicken. I suspected it was meant to be sexy, and yet again I felt sorry for her. I wanted to tell her to stop, that she was making a fool of herself. Blake and Aleks were trying hard not to choke on their laughter. She mouthed what seemed to be 'Duct Tape Lover' at me, and my feelings of benevolence towards her rapidly melted away. I glanced at Blake to see if he'd caught what she'd said and it looked as though he had. His mouth was a tight, flat line and spots of red coloured his cheeks.

Okay, so now a twinge of anger was brewing inside me. She'd made him cross. And usually I was safe here. This was my domain, somewhere I could go and be completely me, losing myself in the music, in singing, and no one could bother me. Now, what with Deborah intent on launching a singing career, I risked bumping into her more often. Unless I asked Georgina downstairs to make sure our sessions were on different days. But even then I'd constantly be on guard, waiting for Deborah to turn up anyway.

I felt selfish and utterly immature, but this was *my* world, not hers, and now she'd managed to invade that too. As if her being at every UK party and seemingly always in my face wasn't enough…

Regardless of my swirling emotions, I smiled kindly at her. She finished her zany dance routine then held one finger up and opened her eyes wide, an exaggerated expression that said, 'Oh, I *knew* there was something I forgot...'

I dreaded to see what she'd do next but braced myself. She wouldn't be able to resist upsetting me some more if her past antics were anything to go by.

She rummaged in a huge red bag that hung over her shoulder. My stomach sank. Memories of a time not so long ago blundered into my head, when she'd delved into her bag at a party and brought out that twenty pence piece.

"You okay?" Blake asked, his voice steely, like he sensed my inner turmoil.

"I will be once she's done whatever it is she plans on doing then leaves." I offered a smile, my attempt to convince him everything was okay.

"She got some kind of beef with you?" Aleks asked.

"It appears so, although I don't know why." I shrugged and watched Deborah pull out a newspaper.

*Oh, bloody hell!*

The front page was covered in a large image of me and Johnny Bravo outside the theatre.

Deborah smiled, transforming her face from spiteful to kind. Then she rushed towards the door. She shoved it open, barging in, and planted herself smack bang in front of Blake.

"So, we meet again," she drawled at him then pushed her breasts out so he could get an even better look.

It turned my stomach into a great big knot. Aleks reached across and squeezed my arm for support. I blinked, wondering how to deal with this situation. I really needed to learn to stand up for myself where she was concerned, but somehow I kept feeling pity for her and it didn't give me the fuel I needed to give her as good as she gave. Besides, why should I turn myself into a bully just to make myself feel better for a couple of minutes?

"So according to this," she said, moving to Blake's side, "our darling Lola is seeing this man here." She held up the newspaper so he could see me and Johnny. "Yet I thought she was seeing you." She lifted one finger to her lips. "Hmm. Unless she's seeing you both?" She fluttered her eyelids. "How do you feel about that, big guy?"

Blake clamped his mouth shut. Was he battling with whether to give her a piece of his mind or ignore her?

"Ah, so you're the strong, silent type, are you?" She half closed her eyes. "I like a man who doesn't say much. A man who lets his actions do the talking."

"Oh, I have plenty to say, ma'am," Blake said. "I'd just prefer not to say it to you."

*Ouch. Ma'am. That had to have stung.*

"I'm twenty-seven, not sixty," she snapped.

I wondered if she thought her antics in the film last night gave her an automatic pass into men's fantasies now. That they'd find her irresistible because of the character she'd been in that film. She'd played a vampire sex kitten and had bared almost all. Maybe that's why she had that corset on now, along with a pair of fishnet stockings and high-heeled shoes. Perhaps her agent or manager had decided she needed to up her sexiness and had urged her to wear something more revealing in her day-to-day life. If David asked me to that, he'd get an outright no.

"Beg your pardon regarding your age," Blake said. "I didn't realise."

Oh, how much did I love him? Infinite amounts, that was how much. His put-downs had been delivered so innocently that they had sounded genuine, but because I knew him, I knew that stare he was giving Deborah wasn't one of appreciation. It was barely concealed anger at her audacity in coming into this room and encroaching on my personal space—and all so she could be horrible to me.

"Anyway," Deborah said, recovering beautifully, plastering a perfect smile on her face and turning to look at me. "I've been so silly." She tittered. "I brought the wrong newspaper with me, although I'm sure I still have the one I meant to bring at home somewhere. Or am I getting confused?" She stared up at the ceiling as though in deep thought. "Hmm. Seems I am. What I meant to bring in here was that magazine on the coffee table out there. The one with another of your men in it."

I was really beginning to get narked at the way she kept implying I slept around. I knew it was her way of putting the seeds of doubt into Blake's head, and I shouldn't have even let her get to me because she had no idea Blake knew everything, but still…

*'Smile and make her think it doesn't bother you,'* Invisible Jenna said, the voice of reason that sometimes piped up when I was feeling unsure and out of my depth.

Jenna had always given the right advice in the past, so I did as I'd been told and smacked on a huge smile, one that I hoped reached my eyes.

"Oh," I said casually, "we saw that when we came in, didn't we, darling?" I willed Blake to agree—I wasn't sure he'd seen the magazine.

Deborah was clearly rubbing it in about Twenny. Did she think that if she spoke about it enough, Blake would ditch me?

"Hmm. The rapper." Blake nodded. "Brilliant way with words."

"Brilliant way with other things too, eh, Lola?" Deborah tittered again.

My smile nearly faltered. "So some people would say."

"Hey, much as this little gathering is nice and all," Aleks said, "we have work to do and you're using up Lola's time here."

*Oh, I could hug him.*

"Just one more thing." Deborah dug her hand into her bag again.

*What now…?*

She pulled her hand out then flipped something at me. My reflexes weren't working properly and I didn't catch whatever she'd thrown. A dull thud sounded, and I looked down at the carpet.

A silver coin rested just in front of my shoe.

I darted my head up to catch Blake's expression. He frowned. He'd missed a trick and it was startlingly obvious he knew it. He squinted, trying to make out how much the coin was worth.

"Oh, a twenty pee." I reached down to pick it up. "Do you remember me telling you, Blake?"

"Ah." He nodded. "I get it now." He laughed, a little too loudly for a little too long.

Deborah stared from me to him then back again. That gesture said it all. 'He even knows about that?' "Right, well…" She tossed her hair, feathers wavering with the movement. "I mustn't take up any more of your time." She strutted to the door, wiggling her bum. "Besides"—she turned to look over her shoulder—"I need to warm up my vocal chords. Real singers do that, you know."

She flounced out of the room with a huge grin on her face, leaving me with an unsettled tummy and Blake with a grin that rivalled hers.

Aleks and Blake shook their heads and whooped with laughter. I watched them, noticing some kind of man-bonding thing going on, and it made me feel so much better. If they could see amusement in what had just happened then so I could I.

I threw off the negativity and laughed with them.

And it felt bloody good.

# 8

## Diary

### Insecure Ingrid

She is a sorry piece of work. Give me strength! Why do I take it so personally? Blake and Aleks seem to know how to laugh her off. Maybe it's because they're men and they don't let that kind of thing bother them? What's my problem? She just really grates on me, that's what it is. How many times have I tried to be nice and give her the benefit of the doubt? Too many. And each time she just throws it back in my face. Perhaps I should stop trying to understand her and stop being kind.

The thing is, though, it's like I can't help but waste valuable energy on resenting this woman. I know the sensible thing to do would be to let go and ignore her every move but I just can't. There's a part of me that feels like if I let my guard down she'll be straight in there, wooing MY man, and I cannot let that happen.

My blood boils at her every move.

Calm down, Charlotte, he loves you. Not her. You. Get a grip. I should feel sorry for her, and I do. Yes, that's it, change your anger and hatred into more pity. That should do the trick. Poor little Bitcherella!

We were due to return to the US soon—or it felt as though it was soon anyway. The days zipped by while I was with Blake, just like they had when I'd first met him. It wouldn't be long before we'd be on a plane and I'd be working over there again. There was a lot to do once we got there, but I was ready to dive in now. David would be coming with us, of course, and Blake had told him he could stay in the apartment I'd been in last time.

I'd be staying in Blake's penthouse because the jobs I had were based in NYC. Whoop-whoop!

As we sprawled out together on my sofa watching a movie—one that wasn't holding my interest at all—I let my mind wander. I was an insecure woman, I knew that, but it annoyed me that I could still be insecure even with Blake in my house. What with Deborah doing her latest thing to unnerve me.

And to top it all, Ginger's comments at Gianni's blundered into my head. He'd said me and Blake shouldn't be together. That we hardly knew one another. It gave me pause to wonder if he could see something that Blake and I couldn't.

*Is this relationship serious? As in, serious-serious?*

Yeah, we'd been through this before, and at the time I'd accepted that we were in it for the long haul but, as was usual with me, I entertained scenarios that would possibly never exist, just so I'd know how to deal with any catastrophes in the future if they should happen.

*Why can't you take each day as it comes and be happy with that? Why do you let other people's words and opinions matter?*

I didn't know why, maybe I was a born worrier. I knew myself well enough that I'd have to sort through my issues in order to make sense of them. And I felt guilty as sin because Blake must have sensed something was up with me and kept asking if anything was wrong. So far I'd responded by kind of snapping, 'No!', but only because I was annoyed at myself for allowing my mind to go down this route. The poor bloke couldn't read my mind so might even think he'd done something to upset me.

No wonder men said women were hard to understand.

My main concern was seeing more of Blake and sorting out where our joint base would be. I so wanted it to be London, but I had a feeling Blake would suggest New York. The problem was, we were both stuck on wanting to remain in our respective homes, and neither of us appeared to want to budge on the subject.

Something had to give, and I couldn't put off the discussion about it any longer.

"So you know when I'm done in the US this time?" I said, wishing I hadn't started the conversation, even though I desperately wanted answers. "Where will we live? I mean, you want us to live together now we're a permanent item, yes?"

Blake turned from watching the TV to look at me. "Of course, but uh…I'm not sure where we should put down roots."

*Oh. Righty ho.* I supposed it depended on his working life. That kind of got my back up, as though his career was more important than mine. Or, as usual, had I jumped to the first conclusion that had sprouted in my head?

"It's just that…" *Stop talking right now. This isn't going to end very well and you know it.* "You know I'm an insecure woman sometimes, right?" *Really, stop talking.* "And no matter how much you compliment me or let me know that you love me, I can't help but think…"

"Think what, Herman?" He smiled, as always, his usual patient self.

And I was going to ruin his good mood, I sensed that, but couldn't seem to stop my runaway mouth.

"Where are we going?" I asked. "I mean, where are we *really* going? What's next? Is this serious? Truly serious?"

He frowned. "Are *you* serious? Asking me that? Come on now, of course this is serious. We've been through all this. I thought we were going to take it as it comes. Just enjoy our time together and sort living arrangements out later when we have to." He reached out for his glass of wine on the coffee table. It didn't stay in the glass for long. He swallowed the lot in one gulp.

*Well done, Charlotte. Way to go with your big mouth.*

"Where has this suddenly come from, anyway?" he asked.

It was on the tip of my tongue to blurt out what Ginger had said but I decided to keep it to myself. Instead, I said, "But you can't just stay at your house, can you?" I cursed myself for bringing this up when we'd been so content watching the film. "When I've done my round of promoting over there, I mean. Could you just stay there while I come back here? Are we going to go down the long-distance-relationship route? Because I kind of thought we'd, you know, move in together at some point. Seeing as we can't stand being apart for very long at any one time. And…and I can't not be with you. I want to be with you all the time. And I know you really love me, so really, would it be that much of an inconvenience for you to set up home here with me?"

My cheeks felt like they were on fire. I knew I'd overstepped the mark somewhere with that verbal diarrhoea, going by the look on his face. He appeared confused, hurt and upset all at once. His eyes had somehow gone darker, and there was a glint in them I didn't like.

*Stop this now before it goes any further.*

"So that's what you expect?" he asked quietly, making intense eye contact.

I squirmed under his scrutiny.

He went on, "That *I'm* the one who must relocate?"

I nodded, biting my bottom lip and thanking my lucky stars that he was getting it. Although he still looked a little angry, and the way he'd spoken…

"I see." He clamped his mouth shut and gave the TV his attention again.

The air bristled with the kind of tension I hadn't wanted to create but had known I would before I'd opened my mouth. Why did I insist on always jumping in without thinking things through properly? I still had so much to learn about life and relationships.

I sighed, annoyed with myself and wondering how I could make things right again. I couldn't think of a thing to say, though, so thought it best to keep quiet. Blake appeared deep in thought, and although he stared at the TV, I knew he wasn't seeing a thing on the screen. I felt awful about ruining the evening.

"I'm sorry," I said. "For being such a pain. I'm not used to how relationships work and I—"

"You know I adore you, don't you?" he said without looking at me. "And that I can't bear the thought of being away from you? That month I spent in hospital with no contact was horrendous. And the times we're not together when you're in the UK or working in other states in the US—or wherever you are in the world. I explained all that. I thought you understood."

I was a very bad person, but God help me, what he'd said about adoring me made me feel on top of the world. Was he going to say we'd live in London? Was he?

"But I have to say this," he continued, "regardless of how you might take it, because it seems you don't quite get some things in life."

He paused, and I held my breath, waiting for the judge's hammer to drop, sending me to the gallows.

"Compromise, Charlotte. It seems to be something you don't comprehend. And seeing the other side of the coin."

Oh. He'd called me Charlotte and not Herman. That wasn't good at all. I opened my mouth to answer then snapped it shut.

*Don't. Don't blurt out a knee-jerk reaction.*

"You're not the only one with an important job," he said, voice hard and showing all too clearly that he wasn't happy. His jaw flickered. "So let me show you the other side of that coin, seeing as you asked me a while back to let you know when you're going 'all selfish' on me. It isn't only you who would have major disruption in shifting your life across the pond. I don't think you appreciate exactly what I do and what it would mean for me to relocate."

So he was saying he wouldn't? I wasn't sure so decided to remain quiet. His words had taken me from my recent high to lower than the depths of Hell. The change in emotions left me feeling sick. *And I only have myself to blame.*

"I have big responsibilities at home," he said, "that are just as important as yours. Like you, I have times where I can't just cast things aside and do whatever I want. I have commitments – people to see, meetings to attend, deadlines to stick to. Yes, I have a competent staff that can oversee the majority, but there are some jobs only I can do. If I manage to secure a business property in the UK and think I can get enough work here to make branching out a solid investment, then I would most definitely live here and find a manager for the American side of things. But I would still have to go to the US to deal with some issues – sometimes for a month or so at a time." He leant forwards to pour more wine. He sipped.

I felt the noose tightening around my neck.

"No different to what you would have to do if you moved to America." He drained his glass again. "There will be times our schedules don't match and you'll be here for months on end and I won't be able to be here with you. So in my mind, it seems reasonable that we don't give up *either* of our homes."

"But I wanted a definite base," I babbled, wishing I'd confessed instead that I'd do whatever it took to make our relationship work. "And you know we're going to fall deeper and deeper in love, don't you, with both of us being stubborn over where we live? Won't that make it even harder if we don't both live at the same address all the time? Are neither of us willing to sacrifice our homes for love?"

"Didn't you hear what I just said?" He sounded calm as anything. "It's like you never heard me. Even if we had a definite base, there will be times we can't both be there at the same time. So it doesn't matter *where* that base is, right?"

I could see what he was saying, and I disliked myself for being so obstinate, but what I'd been trying to get out was that I wanted a home that belonged to *both* of us. A place we'd chosen together. With things inside it that we'd also chosen together. I just couldn't get those words out, though.

*You'd better try because at the moment you're making it worse. Think about what you're saying, how he's hearing it. You sound selfish and unwilling to budge.*

"So we can live in London, yes?" I asked, hopeful.

"Charlotte…" He got up, skirted round the coffee table and headed for the door. He stopped there and looked across at me. "I think it's better that I make myself scarce for a few days. Give you time to be without me so you're reminded what it feels like. Maybe then you'll realise it doesn't matter where we live, so long as we see each other as often as possible." He shook his head. "Remember, you asked me to tell you if you start acting selfish. Well, you're acting selfish. You're a wonderful woman, but man, you're coming across as far from that right now. And it's making me sad."

He left the room. I cringed at the sound of him going upstairs and collecting his stuff together. Now was the time I should get up and go after him, tell him I agreed with him, that I'd do whatever he wanted, but…

I didn't.

I sat where I was and, once the front door closed with such a final, dreadfully quiet click, I blinked away the sting of tears. I didn't want to leave London permanently, didn't think I could.

*Yet when you're in New York, you forget all about it.*

Gosh, I was a bundle of contradictions.

When would I ever learn?

# 9

**Diary**

**What Have I Done?**

Why? Why do I always have to go and balls things up? ☹

It was all going so well. It was like we were on the same page, then suddenly someone changed the storyline on us.

And that someone was me. AGAIN.

I have to get this stuff out of my head and onto the page because then maybe I'll think straight. My thoughts are too crazy and I *know* I'm being selfish—yet I can't see the woods for the bloody trees at the moment. There's a small voice inside me saying that I can't expect him to up sticks and move to the UK permanently. I realise he has a life in America and that me expecting him to move over here is just a ridiculous need. But there's another, louder voice telling me *I* can't just drop it all and uproot to another place.

Yet I'm expecting him to do that for me?

Like I said, I'm selfish. ☹

But isn't that what the Prince Charming is supposed to do—whatever it takes to please his woman? Or is that old-fashioned thinking?

So I need to think about the pros and cons of relocating to New York. If I make a list I might be able to work through it in my head a bit better.

**Cons**

I'll miss Dad, Jenna and Roo-Roo.

I can't just pop to theirs whenever I fancy it for a chat.

I know there's the phone or email but it isn't the same.

The little shop on the corner is so convenient. (Okay, I'm really stretching it with this one.)

And I'll miss the little man who owns it. (All right, all right…)

They might not have Phish Food ice cream over there. (I'm not checking on Google – at this point in time it's a valid con so that's the end of that.)

I don't want to leave my house. It's the first one I've ever owned. (Yes, there are better houses out there, but I happen to be in love with this one.)

**Pros**

I'll see more of Blake.

They might have better ice cream. (Is that even possible?)

Blake's penthouse is gorgeous.

A new house together would be gorgeous.

I'll rarely see Deborah Cressida at parties. (Unless her career flies worldwide and she takes it upon herself to torment me across the pond too.)

I'll see more of Blake.

I can have more fun – there's more to do there.

I'll see more of Blake.

Dad and Jenna can have brilliant holidays with us.
I'll see more of Blake.

So, that's the list. I'm sure there's more I could put on it but I'm trying not to be too negative. But there's that voice again, saying, 'I didn't work my butt off, take myself from the streets to the stage to let the first person I fall in love with tell me what do and when to do it!'

Is that what's really bugging me, then? Being told what to do?

But he hasn't exactly told me what to do.

What sort of person does that make me sound?

I don't need to answer that. I already know. ☹

I want to follow Blake—not in a stalkerish manner, you understand, that would just be wrong. I want to be near him all the time, but I just can't leave it all behind and pretend that England doesn't matter and that I don't want to stay.

Jenna would say if I loved him I'd be willing to do anything to be with him.

And she'd be right.

But—and there's that voice *again*—he should want to do the same for me.

So why *can't* we elope to America? What is it that's really stopping me? Am I afraid, is that it? All I've known for most of my life is London. Maybe that's what it is—the fear of going over there for good and hating it once the novelty factor goes away?

But I loved it when I had my holiday and worked there…

Argh! I'm getting on my own nerves.

Okay. Let me look at this logically. He only works in an office, he doesn't need to be in a particular place—at least that's what I've gathered from what he's told me. He's the boss, other people do everything for him, so he could work from his laptop, maybe? From anywhere? And what about this… It's not rocket science—like he said, he could just set up a new office in London and work from there. He said he could get an American manager.

Yes! That's exactly what he could do!

Perhaps I'm right after all and I don't need to budge on this one. The guy follows the girl, not the other way around, right? Although he did follow me this far already… And David does think I should start spending more time in the States…

So if I want to give my relationship with Blake a proper chance then I should be prepared to live with him over there.

This is confusing.

Okay, it's make a decision time. I'm going to write my final answer down and stick with it.

Here it is. We should live in the UK. I won't give in!

**Diary**

**Giving In**

Okay, so I said I wouldn't give in.

I lied.

I've woken up this morning with a completely different outlook on things. I have no idea why I was so stubborn about this whole mess. If I live in America, I can still fly back for any work I'm doing in England. And to be honest, I'd love to spend some more time in the States anyway and build my career there. Flying back and forth like I have been is messing with my face. I'm getting handbags under my eyes. Deep down I still feel that Prince Charming should be willing to follow his princess wherever she is and be at her beck and call, but is that reality?

No, it bloody isn't. And I'm an independent woman. I've done this on my own so far without a man, so how come I've developed old-fashioned ideals? Have I let my fantasies take over just a little bit too much?

I think so.

Plus, if Blake gave in to my every whim and followed me around like a helpless puppy dog, would I find that attractive? Definitely not! He's got fire and spirit—who am I to come along and take that away from him? Those traits are a part of him and, let's face it, after I read up on the Internet last night what kind of thing the head of a large company actually does, I'll admit to being ashamed of myself.

No, he can't just work from his laptop anywhere, not in the construction business. It's me who can work from either location without much hassle.

So... Yeah, it's not really giving in, more like owning up.

To the fact that I was wrong.

Now I need to find the courage to tell him that.

EDIT: I just put this diary away then had to come back. What am I on about, finding the courage? What am I, a mouse?

I have the courage. I'm big enough and brave enough to admit when I'm wrong. I just had a silly little wobble, that's all. I can do this. I can move away from London. It'll still be here, and if I get homesick when I'm not working in the UK, I can jump on a plane and come for a visit.

Okay. That's sorted, then.

I feel better now. ☺

I had some rare time off in between my projects in the UK and the States, and that was good because when the chips were down, there was only one thing for it. A tub of Ben & Jerry's Phish Food and a dose of *Muriel's Wedding*. It was my favourite feel-sorry-for-myself film. It usually upped my spirits, made me laugh and see life in a different light. My comfy granny pants, T-shirt and snugly tracksuit bottoms completed the picture, and I curled up onto the sofa to forget the world and my troubles for an hour or so.

Halfway through the film my eyes drooped. I'd been awake quite a bit during the night, so it wasn't surprising I was tired. I blinked to stop myself falling asleep but the pull to the land of slumber was too hard to resist and I let myself drift off…only to be rudely awakened by a loud banging on the front door. I opened my eyes to find my spoon stuck to my top along with a soggy, melted lump of ice cream.

"Oh, bum!"

I hauled myself off the sofa, the spoon going flying and landing on the rug. I set the ice cream tub on the coffee table then staggered to the front door in a daze, trying to snap myself out of sleep mode but failing miserably. It was probably only Roo-Roo at the door anyway, and he wouldn't mind seeing me in this state. The letterbox flapped open, and whoever stood behind the glass bent down.

"That's it, Herman, we're going!"

*Blake?*

"I won't leave things like this," he said, a breeze of cold air wafting inside.

I smiled, wide awake now. Pretending to be annoyed, I said, "Oh, won't you now?"

"No, I won't. I don't care if you move or don't move. All I know is that I won't make this trip home without you. I want you to come back with me now, see New York again while you have some time off, before you have to start work again over there, then tell me you can't live there. I remember how happy you were, how you looked like you belonged there. And another thing, I refuse to stop banging on the door until you agree to come with me."

As though to get his point across fully, he stood upright and started knocking. Okay, so I'd made out I was a little annoyed with Blake, what with our argument last night, but deep down I was delighted. My heart was doing a hop, skip and a jump. My Prince Charming had come to whisk me off my feet and he wouldn't take no for an answer!

Maybe that was all I'd wanted. Maybe I'd needed him to make the decision for me—because I didn't have the nerve to make it for myself.

"Stop that a moment," I said loudly so he could hear me over his crazy knocking. "Just give me a few minutes to think about this."

I didn't need a few minutes. I didn't even need a second. I legged it upstairs and into my bedroom, tossing whatever clean stuff I could fit into my largest suitcase, hoping the weight of it wouldn't go over at the airport. I all but ripped off my tracksuit, throwing on a pair of jeans and a tight-fitting T-shirt. I grabbed my passport out of my bedside drawer then dragged my suitcase down the stairs, the bump of it on every step reminding me of how my bum had felt as I'd slid down them when Johnny Bravo had come to call.

Had that really been a year or so ago? It seemed like a lifetime.

In the hallway, I jammed my arms into my jacket, shouting, "Just give me another minute!" while Blake hammered away at the door. My neighbours would probably think there was a domestic dispute going on, but I didn't care. I felt free, excited, and that I was doing the right thing. I laughed while racing round the house, securing windows and doors. I found my handbag wedged down the side of the sofa and slung it over my shoulder, pounding back into the hallway out of breath and so light of spirit that I might well float up to the ceiling. I jammed my feet into a pair of beige Ugg boots and, at last, I was as ready as I would ever be.

After taking a deep lungful of air then letting it out, I swished open the front door.

And launched myself into Blake's arms.

"I'm coming with you. I'm sorry," I blurted. "I'm so selfish, I couldn't see straight, and… Oh, bloody hell, just kiss me, will you?"

He swung me out of the house and around in a circle, kissing me silly and making everything bad go away. How had I thought I could be stubborn and stay here while he lived thousands of miles away? How had I thought I could live without him for any length of time?

He ended the kiss and plopped me back down. We stared at each other, panting, both smiling, and my heart—oh, wow, my heart was beating like crazy.

"Forget the argument, right?" he said. "Just forget the whole thing as though it never happened. We need each other, plain and simple. So we're going to work this out—so *both* of us are happy with whatever we arrange, you got that?"

I nodded, smiling, feeling goofy but not caring one bit. He held me tightly, scrunched up into him as though he never wanted to let me go. And I didn't want him to. How easily I'd forgotten what it had been like when I'd come home from America in the past, when it seemed we'd split up. I'd been a right state, moping around, getting drunk and crying on Roo-Roo's shoulder.

To think I could have been doing that all over again!

My Blake was here, and he was willing to do whatever it took.

And so was I. Finally, so was I.

# 10

According to the taxi driver, the ride to the airport wouldn't take too long. We didn't care. Besides, we were too busy kissing and making up for our silly spat. I'd managed to give David a ring as we'd set off, letting him know I was going to America a couple of days early. I was glad I didn't have any more jobs on in the UK this week, otherwise I'd have been in deep trouble. Plus, I couldn't have gone if I had commitments. I wouldn't have wanted to let anyone down.

Then it hit me, what Blake had been saying. *He* couldn't let anyone down either. Bloody hell, I'd been such a beast to him—and I'd known it at the time too. I needed to grow up. Seriously grow up.

"I'm so very sorry," I whispered against his neck. "If I ever act so unreasonable again, just tell me straight, okay? For all the good it will do you, because I didn't listen last time you said I'd been acting selfish." It might sting a bit, but if he didn't tell me off about this kind of thing, I'd end up losing him. I couldn't expect anyone to put up with those kinds of demands.

"Hey, it's okay. At least you saw the light." He kissed the top of my head. "In the end."

"Oi!" I playfully slapped his chest. "I feel so wicked for what I did."

"And so you should."

I heard the smile in his voice, but really, it wasn't funny. And the fact that he was prepared to forgive me—again—for my behaviour only served to point out that I needed to take a step back sometimes and see things from all sides instead of just my own.

*See the other side of the coin.*

"It won't happen again," I mumbled, ashamed of myself.

"Oh, I'm sure it will, Herman. You're headstrong. Overly needy sometimes. I doubt you'll be able to change as easily as you think."

I was about to protest the needy comment but resisted. After all, I'd just told him to give it me to straight. Instead of arguing the toss, I kissed him madly, wanting to forget all about this silliness and start over on a clean page. He kissed me back with passion, and the taxi driver said, "Blimey, get a room, you two!"

His words broke any remaining tension, and we pulled apart, laughing like there was no tomorrow. Laughing so hard my tummy ached. It felt so good to be back on track, and I promised myself—and Blake, silently—that I'd honest-to-goodness meant what I'd said.

No more being selfish.

The airport loomed ahead, and instead of taking the usual route to the main car park, the driver turned off, steering us down a road I didn't recognise. He parked up beside what looked like a little old lady's house—a cottage—an adjacent runway streaking off into the distance. I glanced at Blake, raising my eyebrows in question. He smiled in answer then got out, helping the driver lift our bags from the boot. I joined them, staring down the runway, assuming I'd got it wrong and it was just another road.

Blake picked up our cases, and I followed him into the house. We walked through a short hallway into what would have been a living room. Three security men stood inside, eyeing us as though we'd done something wrong. Or maybe they'd been trained to stare at people that way, scaring them witless. I was the same whenever I saw a policeman. I tried to act nonchalant so they'd know by my expression that I was a good girl and they didn't need to pull me over in my car or arrest me on the street.

I grew paranoid, thinking we were going to be strip-searched or something, my mind doing that thing it did, which resulted in messing with my nerves. Every movie I'd seen where the characters were falsely accused of trying to smuggle drugs went through my head. Someone could have been hiding in the boot of the taxi, unpicking the sewn edge of the suitcase lining and sliding a shifty package in there before concealing it. Or something along those lines.

"What's happening?" I whispered to Blake, thoughts running riot, showing me images of Blake being the head of some secret organisation, not construction, and he'd committed a crime for which he needed to go to prison. This, right here in the little house, was the sting, where his true self would be revealed and I'd be swept to the floor in the scuffle, screaming out my love for Blake through my hair—it would be all over my face in knots—and declaring that I'd wait for him to serve his time, true to him until the end.

*Oh, for the love of…*

I clamped my thoughts in place, preventing them from speeding and causing havoc. Blake looked at me as if I'd gone mad.

"What's up?" he asked. "You've gone a little pale."

"This," I hissed. "Them!" I darted my eyes to the right to indicate the uniformed men.

"We're checking in, sweetheart, that's all. Don't celebrities in England have to go through security?"

He handed over his passport, so I did the same, my hand trembling.

"Well, yes, but not like this." Confused more than ever, I frowned. "I just go through the same as everyone else. In the main airport."

Blake winked. "Not when you travel with me, you don't."

A floor-vibrating rumble shook through the building, and I instinctively grabbed Blake's arm. I held in a squeal of fright, my nerves so taut I thought they might snap any minute and I'd end up a quivering, snotty mess.

*Calm down. One of the jumbo jets must have landed or something.*

"Thank you, sir," one of the men said, handing our passports back, unperturbed by the violent roaring swallowing the cottage. "All clear."

*Okay, so Blake isn't a secret spy.*

Blake slipped the passports into his pocket then waited for our cases to go along a short conveyer belt then through a scanning machine. The luggage plopped out of the other side, winging its way back to us on a mini carousel. The rumble got more aggressive, adding to my unease. It felt like I was in a warzone and bombs would rain down any second.

"Have a safe journey," Uniform Bloke said and lifted one hand to wave.

"Thank you," I stuttered, feeling all kinds of novice.

Back outside, I was startled to see a large jet occupying the runway with a crew of four standing beside its lowered steps. Blake carried our cases towards it, but I stood there, trying to comprehend what was going on.

"Hey, sir," a crewman said. He slapped Blake on the back.

*Bit familiar, isn't he?*

"Hey yourself, Francis." Blake jerked a thumb at the cases. "Two this time."

I continued to stare. Wow. I knew Blake had money, but I didn't know he had his own jet and crew. How on earth hadn't that conversation come up over the past year? Had I been that busy there hadn't been time to discuss these things? I was gobsmacked and so excited, wondering if the journey wouldn't take as long if this jet flew faster than a jumbo.

Pushing myself forward, I followed Blake up the steps and into a plane that looked more like a living room than an aircraft. The seats were similar to sofas, and the floor was carpeted with thick pile. Blake grinned, clearly enjoying my shock.

"Nice, right?" he asked, using one of our joke words. Nice.

"Awesome," I breathed. I sat on a three-seater sofa adjacent to the window then snapped on my seatbelt.

The stairs were lifted, the door closed, and Blake and I were alone. This was so weird, being the only passengers. He settled beside me, belted up, then took my hand.

"This is the proper way to travel." He smiled wide. "And I can't think of anyone I'd rather travel with."

Oh, he'd only gone and melted my heart again. I was so bloody lucky.

In no time at all we took off, and once we'd removed our seatbelts, it didn't feel as though we were in a plane at all. The pilot's voice came out from a hidden speaker somewhere, and he advised us to get some rest.

"I wasn't thinking of resting," Blake whispered as the lights went down to faint pinpricks and automatic blinds covered the windows.

"Ooh!" I jumped and skewed sideways. The darkness wasn't absolute, but it was close. I fumbled to find his hand, to orientate myself, breathing heavily as what he had in mind began to sink in.

He slid one hand beneath my T-shirt, and I was lost already. He kissed me softly, almost reverently, and I floated in a swirl of happiness and security. Once again I chastised myself for being so stubborn, for causing arguments that hadn't needed to happen, and wondered if deep down I liked the making-up experience afterwards. But putting us through the pain and upset beforehand? No, surely I didn't like that.

I shifted so I was on my side, full length on the sofa. He nestled next to me, our chests touching. I slid one of my hands over his side and down to the bottom of his back, content to just kiss and let the emotions it produced wash over me.

He brushed soft pecks on my cheeks, my eyelids, my nose. I held my breath—the air seeming to fizzle around us—and listened to the thud of my pulse and the banging of my heart. That heart held all my love for him, and I wondered how such a big thing could fit in there. How I could have thought that walking away from him had been the right decision. With us being here like this, it was abundantly obvious we belonged together. Everything felt so *right* with him close, when my emotions did the talking instead of my mind. Maybe I should listen to my heart in future and not those silly little voices that always ill-advised me?

"I love you so much," he whispered into my ear. He drew his hand out from under my T-shirt to pop the button on my jeans. "Missed you."

His breath tickled, and a shiver of anticipation wafted up my spine. I couldn't reply—I was too busy loving what he was doing—and as my jeans and underwear were eased down, I kicked off my Uggs while undressing him. His clothes clonked to the floor, as did his shoes. We tangled our legs together, kissing away.

He shifted me onto my back, covering my body with his, and our connection had me hiking in a short, quick breath. I wanted the lights to go up so I could see him, to look into his eyes and know what he was feeling, to read his intentions on how the next few minutes would pan out.

But I didn't really need light. It was clear he wanted the slow approach, a gentle union that expressed everything he felt without having to be rough about it. I stroked his back beneath his shirt, cupping my hands over his shoulder blades, clutching him. In our dark, secluded void, I surrendered myself, fully relaxing. Between kisses, he murmured things, beautiful things that swelled my heart—and then I knew how all that love fitted in there.

I held him tighter, and my heart rate picked up, thrumming along, and I floated on love and being loved.

"Perfect," he whispered. "You're perfect."

I smiled as he kissed me, feeling so lucky, so wanted, warm and safe. Before Blake there had been nothing like this and there would *only* be this with him. We rested, still, the only movement our chests from staggered breathing and the need to get it under control.

With my face buried in the crook of his neck, there was nowhere else I'd rather have been. Nowhere I needed to be. The world could disappear and I wouldn't care.

While the plane hummed and turbulence sent it slightly off-balance, I held Blake to me, for once not desperate to fill the silence with my usual verbal assaults. This quiet time, this moment of reflection, was perhaps the best thing for both of us. I wondered what he was thinking and wished I could read his mind. Was he as happy as me? Was he so pleased he'd spirited me to his plane—and that I'd even agreed to go with him?

I liked to think so.

He snuggled beside me, and I stared at the muted lights, likening them to stars. It was as though we were on a bed outside, the stars the only witness to what we'd just done. I'd keep this memory in my head forever. My heart and soul were at peace, and if only real life and my silly thoughts didn't have to be so rude and butt in, I'd feel like this for the rest of my life.

**Diary**

**Just a Quick Note!**

I am the luckiest girl in the world. Eek! My man just whisked me away in his private jet and loved me like he should. Bliss! Eternal happiness! The universe has stopped still and it's just me and my Blake. How can life get any better? How was I living before I met him? I simply can't imagine ever getting on a normal plane again now, not after travelling in such private style. This isn't just a flight, it's a magical, fairy tale dream that Walt Disney himself couldn't have conjured up in one of his stories. People wouldn't have believed it!

Step aside, Julia Roberts, I'm the new *Pretty Woman* in town. And it's actually happening, it isn't some romance movie. Aaaahhhhh!

And to top it all off, we're now descending into the city that never sleeps. Blake, me, and a gigantic aeroplane window showcasing the city at its best. Buzzing lights, the Empire State Building beaming bright, and the millions of specks that are people enjoying the city.

Wow. What a view!

Leaving now, must dash off my private jet with my man, and lay beside him for the next however long, pinching myself!

# 11

We settled into Blake's penthouse, and it was as though I'd never left America. I should have known this would happen and, hopefully for the last time, cursed myself a blue streak for digging my heels in over where we should live. Then I got on with unpacking, putting my things in his wardrobe and drawers, my toiletries in his bathroom. Afterwards, I mooched around his living room, loving the sunken area in the centre, which was like a cosy den with the way the leather sofas hugged three of the walls. The lovely rug in the middle was heaven on my bare toes, and I dropped to the floor to roll around on it.

Blake came in, looked down at me from one side of the raised area, and shook his head. "This is why I love you so much. You're insane!"

I laughed, and when he came to join me, we messed about together, making out a little and getting all hot and flustered.

Coming up for air, I said, "What was your childhood dream?"

"That's easy." He stroked my hair back from my face. "I wanted to be a DJ."

I cracked up at that, imagining him spinning records on decks and encouraging partygoers to freak out like they'd never freaked out before. "Check one two, DJ B in da house!"

"Yeah, yeah, you laugh it up, woman."

"What would you wear?" I asked. "A tight-fitting vest and skinny jeans?" I laughed even harder. "A massive medallion?"

"Whatever. Get it out of your system. I'll wait."

It took a while for me to stop giggling at images of him with huge earphones on and shouting into the mic that the crowd needed to *hype it up* when he played his next song.

"Okay. You done now?"

I nodded.

"Now it's your turn. What's your favourite childhood memory?"

"Ah, that's easy too. Every Christmas, Dad would wrap up a tangerine as a present and me and Jenna always knew what it was but pretended to guess like we had no idea." I smiled at the recollection. "Now I look back, I think Dad must have known we knew, but he never said anything either. It was like our little ritual."

"Why give you a tangerine?"

"Because Dad said that was the only present *his* dad had got the first year after the war, and it was the best present ever. I think he got the same present as a kid—you know, my granddad showing him what life used to be like—and Dad wanted us to appreciate the other gifts we had. So we learned to be grateful."

"He sounds a good guy." Blake twirled a lock of my hair around his finger.

"He is. You need to meet him and Jenna soon. All this crazy hopping between countries, and our schedules…it seems mad that so much time has passed and I haven't taken you over to meet them." I knew they'd love Blake.

"Yeah, and you need to meet the rest of my family too."

*If they're anything like Ginger, I don't think I want to…*

"So tell me about them. I've met Connor, but you have a sister too, don't you?"

"Yeah, but I'm an only child really." He sighed. "I haven't spoken about this to many people, but I can't expect you to be with me and not know the truth. I mean, we've been together a while now so there's no reason to keep this stuff back." He took a deep breath then let it out again. "My mother died when I was five. My dad? Well, he took off, couldn't stand being without her. Apparently I wasn't enough for him to stick around for. So he arranged for me to go live with the Beasleys—they were childhood friends of his. Patrick and Dylis, except I call them Pat and Dyl. Connor was a school pal of mine, so it wasn't so bad living with them."

"Oh my goodness! Your mother. I had no idea. And you being left like that. I don't know what to say."

I hugged him tight, rubbing his back and feeling rotten for him. No wonder he had trust and love issues. No wonder he'd said he didn't let himself love new people often because he feared getting hurt or left. That kind of trauma in his childhood must have cut right down to the bone.

"There isn't much to say, sweetheart," he said. "It's done, and I've had a good life. Spent a lot of time with Pat in his garage, learning how to build things. He's in construction too, and he taught me the basics and gave me the drive to run my own business. I owe them so much. The pair of them treat me like their own son. I couldn't have asked for more."

He cleared his throat, and I looked from his face to his Adam's apple. It bobbed erratically, and I had the idea a change of subject might be in order but I didn't know what to say. If I switched themes, it would make me seem as though I was brushing off his heartache and I didn't want that.

"So," he said. "That's enough of that. You see that painting up there?"

He pointed to a large canvas on the ceiling. It was a huge skyline of New York when the Twin Towers had been there—and it was beautiful. Black and white, very striking. And haunting.

"It's lovely," I said. "It took me a few visits before I noticed it. Bet it cost a fortune, didn't it?"

"Nope. Only the cost of the canvas and oils. I painted it."

I jerked my head back to look at him. "*You* painted it?"

Another thing I hadn't known about him—well, he'd told me he dabbled with painting, but I had no idea he was this good. Maybe Ginger was right after all. I didn't know Blake enough.

He nodded. "Dyl taught me when I was young. She's a great artist with the patience of a saint. She had to have patience to teach me. Took me a long time to learn to just let it go and relax while creating instead of forcing it."

"Wow…"

"I ate so many darn Red Vines while making that picture." He chuckled.

"Red Vines?" I frowned. "Never heard of them."

"Red liquorice. I've got some in the kitchen, so you can try them, if you want." He paused, then, "My sister got me hooked on them. Connor's sister. She used to share hers when we were kids. She always looked out for me. You know, when people meet her, they think she's bossy, a little in your face, but underneath all that she's soft. I think she took it upon herself to help mother me." He laughed quietly, staring up at his painting. "When I was a little boy, I used to love Superman. Anyway, Dyl had this grand collection of Swarovski crystals—something Pat saved religiously for so he could buy her a small one every few years. I always had my eye on a green one, which I swear I believed was Kryptonite. One day, Dyl left the crystal cabinet unlocked and during an intense imaginary play time as Superman, I took the crystal out and kind of ruined it. I'd made scratches and tiny chips all over it from throwing it around."

"Oh. My. Word."

"Uh-huh. I didn't realise how much they cost—or, more importantly, how the monetary value wasn't what was important to Dyl. It was the sentimental value. So after I saw what I'd done I immediately regretted it because yeah, I knew I'd be in serious trouble with Pat. But my sister came home before they did—they'd been out someplace, can't remember where—and she saw how worried I was. She grabbed that crystal off me, and when Pat and Dyl got back, she took the entire blame for what had happened."

"What, she told them she'd been pretending to be Superman?" I almost laughed. Jenna would have done that.

"No, they wouldn't have swallowed that one. She was a Barbie girl, through and through. She said she was dusting for her mom and accidently dropped it. Thinking back, I have no idea why they believed that. Dropping the crystal once wouldn't have produced the mess it was in. Maybe they realised she'd been covering for me and decided not to say anything. Ever since then she continued to take the fall for me—still tries to at times. I keep telling her she needs to butt out a bit now I'm grown, but she doesn't listen. So when you meet her, maybe me telling you this will help you to understand the way she acts sometimes. Like she has to protect me from people. Like she has to protect me from you."

*So the sister and Ginger both feel the need to intrude on Blake's relationships, then?* "I understand. And I'll try to bear that in mind."

"Tell me something about you? Another memory, perhaps? We don't have enough times like this—together in person, anyway—where we can just talk and get to know each other more."

"I don't know about a memory, but I will tell you that right up until I became famous I was scared of the dark. Still am sometimes, but it isn't as bad as it was. There was a time when the thought of being alone in the dark and not being able to see past my nose was my biggest fear. I had a night light at home, right into my early twenties."

"So up until a couple of years ago then?"

I blushed. "Mmm."

"So how come you don't need a night light anymore?"

"Because I had to learn to walk to the Underground platforms at night. So, okay, there were street lights, but you know what I mean—walking there was something I had to do. One time I was so tired when I got home that I forgot to put on my little lamp, and from then on I didn't bother. Besides, you came along, didn't you, so I'm safe now."

"I'll always keep you safe, Herman. Always. For as long as you want me to."

He pulled me closer, stroking my hair and kissing my temple. I closed my eyes, loving this moment and that we'd shared some more things about ourselves. It kind of felt like I was proving Ginger wrong—that me and Blake *did* belong together. We were growing much closer, and someday soon we'd have no more secrets and memories to talk about because we'd have shared them all.

"You want a Red Vine?" he asked.

"Do you?"

"Yeah, talking about them has given me the urge."

"All right, so long as you can bear to part with one."

He sat up then stood, holding out his hand. I took it, and he helped me up, leading me towards the kitchen.

"I'd give you the whole tub," he said and let go of my hand to rummage in one of the cupboards. "*That's* how much I love you."

"The whole tub, eh?" I cocked my hip, striking a pose that was meant to challenge what he'd said.

"Yep, the whole tub."

I grinned at him, and after he'd peeled off the lid, I reached inside and pulled out a liquorice. I took a bite, and oh yeah, I could see myself getting hooked on them too.

"You love them, right?" He laughed.

"I do," I said and gave him a big fat hug. "But I love you more."

**Diary**

**Nobody's Perfect**

Painting! Well, that wasn't on my perfect-man list but it is now. Who'd have thought he was such an excellent artist? I have to give the boy credit, he's really good at it and I wouldn't say no to hanging one of his creations in my hallway. As he certainly doesn't paint by numbers, maybe he could create a cityscape of London from a photograph. That would be so cool.

I just wish I could paint too. We could become an artistic duo, taking the world by storm with our awesome canvases.

I hope he doesn't get me a tangerine for Christmas! Saying that, it would be quite sweet, really.

Hmm, what if I buy him one of those crystals? A green one, so he could always have a smile on his face when he looked at it, remembering his Superman days. Actually, that might not be a good idea. He'd been upset about scratching Dylis' one. The memory might still be one of those raw ones that hurts every time he thinks about it.

There's so much I still need to learn about him. So much yet to share. And his sister—Ginger's sister… Blake hasn't even told me her name. I have to wonder about that. Oh well, nobody's perfect. He might have just forgot. And when will I meet her? We might become really good friends. That would be nice, but I'm not expecting much on that score, not after what Blake said about her. If she's majorly protective, she might hate me on sight. That would be awkward.

Isn't it strange that when you fall in love with someone, you don't just fall in love with them? There's a whole load of people you have to meet, get to know, and hope they like you. If it was just a case of me loving Blake and him loving me, we'd have no problems at all. But the world and its wife always have a habit of thinking they need to intervene.

Sometimes, I could shout, 'Leave us alone! We don't need anyone else!'

But we do. I still need Dad and Jenna, and I definitely need Roo-Roo from time to time.

Wow, this is a bit of a long entry, isn't it! But Blake's asleep and I can't stare at him all night, much as I'm tempted. If he woke up and caught me he'd think I was even more of a weirdo than I already am. Or maybe not. I've caught him looking at me when he thinks I can't see him.

Oh, I'm *so* lucky. I'm hyped up on love! Super-charged with devotion! Yeah! ☺

Okay, time for bed.

EDIT: Back again! I tried to sleep but Blake did this snoring thing, where he didn't snore with snorts but kind of like a puff of air that made a cute little noise. I had to write it down because it was so sweet and I didn't want to forget it.

Right. Really going to bed now. Byeeeeeeeeeeee! ☺

# 12

David has been in talks with an American basketball team about me being the next face of one of their sportswear brands, which would further build my profile in the US. After a few days off spent cosied up in Blake's penthouse, I was ready for today's work, which was attending a game to show my support. It would be an exciting thing for me to do, because basketball was like netball in a way—wasn't it?—and I'd always enjoyed that at school. I also had to sing at half-time, which I was really looking forward to.

Blake was allowed to come with me—*another* exciting thing about it—and he'd get to meet some of his idols. He'd apparently met some stars, what with him building *that* sports stadium—the one where that famous woman was meant to have been the face of his venture but instead had taken a huge chunk of his money.

We arrived in one of Blake's cars, some sleek number that reminded me of a Mercedes, the driver dropping us off around the back of the venue. A man met us outside at one of the doors, ushering us in with so much enthusiasm I wondered if he ever experienced down days. I didn't think so and decided I should adopt his happy-go-lucky attitude more often. I'd been a Debbie Downer too much of late, and now that me and Blake had sorted out the housing issue—or rather, I'd woken up about it—the sky was the limit.

"This is surreal," I said, looking round for the other man who was supposed to be meeting us.

"I'd have thought you'd be used to this kind of thing by now." Blake slid his arm around my shoulder as we walked over to a gleaming reception desk.

"Things like this…I don't think I'll ever get used to them."

A muscle man sat behind the desk, and because it was made from glass I saw he had shorts on to go with the vest top covering his broad chest. His ankle socks were bright white against his tanned skin, and a pair of trainers covered his huger than huge feet. He must have been a size thirteen or so, and they resembled boats moored on an ocean of tiles. He stood, rising to around a hundred feet tall, and I sucked in a breath at the size of him. Who was this massive creature?

"Hey." He came out from behind the desk. "Lola, right? I recognise you from the pictures."

I didn't know what pictures he was talking about but smiled and nodded. "Yes, that's me, and this is Blake—"

"Mr Hudson, good to see you, man!"

Mr Skyscraper slapped Blake on the back, dwarfing him as he stood by his side.

*Oh. So they know one another?*

Blake gave me a wink. "Meet SJ Stevens, aka Slam 'Em Stevens, one of the best basketball players on the planet. Good friend of mine."

Oh, the little bugger hadn't let me in on *that* secret.

I nudged him in the ribs with my elbow. "Why didn't you say?"

"Because you were giddy with happiness when you told me you'd got this job and I didn't want to spoil it at the time." He grinned.

"Hey now," Mr Skyscraper said. "No bickering on my account. Come on, I'll take you to the court. The other players are warming up right now. Cheerleaders too. And those cheerleaders love Blake."

*Whump.* There went a snap of jealousy smacking into my gut but I whacked it away as quickly as it had come. *No need to feel that way.*

"He's pulling your leg," Blake whispered as we followed the human building down a glass-roofed corridor. "I've never met them."

The sound of training shoes squeaking on a polished wooden floor and women chanting out a mantra had my tummy exploding with anticipation. The man mountain turned left and stepped aside in a doorway so we could enter first. We came out in an aisle between the stands, the many chairs rising either side of us, reminding me of Wembley Arena. I caught a glimpse of a slice of court ahead and followed SJ and Blake to the edge of it, staring out at the players as they ducked, dived and dodged. They were all huge, making me feel super small, like a Polly Pocket doll beside a regular human.

"You want to go up on the stands and watch?" SJ asked. He pointed at the rows of chairs to our right. "Then when the proper game starts, you can move on into one of the private boxes."

A private box!

"Thanks, man," Blake said. "You going to practise?"

"Yeah." Mr Skyscraper nodded so deep I expected his head to roll off. "Plan to win this sucker today."

He loped away, curiously graceful on the court considering his height, and caught the ball as it was thrown to him then slammed it into the net. It didn't surprise me—it wasn't like he had far to jump to get it in.

I followed Blake up some stairs to the seats, having to turn sideways once we got to a row halfway up because the aisles were so narrow. I went to pull down the seat part of a chair, struggling a bit—the mechanism that held it was rather strong—but with a good yank I was able to press it into place. I had to keep hold of it, though—it wanted to ping right back up again.

"Here, try this one," Blake said.

I shuffled along, but that seat was the same. "They're probably all like it."

With a flurry of faffing about, I managed to sit down, albeit flustered and hot. The players were all cavorting around on one half of the court, while a group of pretty women did a dance routine, their leotards and leggings fitting them snugly. They waved their arms above their heads in perfect sync, and I marvelled at how not one of them stepped out of line.

I'd never been a dancer—all gangly arms and legs and no co-ordination—so when I watched someone who could dance, I had nothing but respect for them. The desire was there for me, just not the execution, and I told people my inner freak-to-the-tunes gene had got buried beneath the singing one.

"Two, four, six, eight, who do we appreciate?"

I appreciated Blake, but I didn't think that's what they meant.

"Grand Stars, they totally rule, we just think they're mighty cool!"

Their chant made me think of Twenny Pee and his cringeworthy raps, and I hid a shudder, squashing the memory of me and him right down into the depths of my mind.

"Lola, we want you now! Come dance with us, we'll show you how!"

Oh dear. They hadn't just said that, had they?

Blake nudged me with his shoulder. "Off you go."

"No, really, I don't do dancing."

Nerves exploded in my belly, and I shifted on the seat. My backside left it momentarily, lifting a few inches, and the chair took that moment, while all eyes were on me, to snap upwards. My body folded within its gripping embrace, my bum falling into the gap between the seat and the back rest. Like before, when I'd been trapped in the bush, my arms and legs stuck upwards, and I imagined they and my head were all Blake could see. I shifted my eyes across to look at him, to plead for help while mewling and trying to pop myself out again. He was doing his best not to laugh, I could tell, and if this wasn't me trapped like a rodent in the jaws of death, I'd have wanted to laugh too.

"Help?" I squeaked.

I jiggled in an attempt to propel myself up and out, but my vigorous jerking of hips only served to send my bum lower. I felt the cold touch of the floor, and panic truly set in, with me thinking I'd be stuck there for good—or until a group of firemen came along with their equipment to cut me out with those metal saw things.

"Here, take hold of my hands." Blake stood in front of my sandwiched self and held his arms out.

"I would if I could, but you can see how it is here."

He grasped my fingers and pulled.

"Wait! Oh, oh, wait!" I wanted to compose myself, to at least try to exit the Chair Beast with some style and finesse. Mind you, there wasn't exactly a graceful way to get out of a situation like this. I was horrified, knowing everyone on court was probably staring, and I considered staying down here until they'd all gone.

"Ready now?" Blake asked.

I nodded as best I could, and he tugged my hands. My bum was stuck fast, so I wiggled again, thinking of how corks came out of champagne bottles if you did that. One forceful yank from Blake had me indeed popping out of that bottle. The chair seat lowered, my feet touched the floor, then the chair snapped up again, the edge of it kissing my backside as if reminding me it could have scoffed me almost whole again. Blake steadied me as I teetered on my high heels, while I wished I hadn't worn them now that my legs had gone wobbly. I nestled my face in his chest, as though doing that would make everyone else disappear, and he rubbed my back.

"You okay?" he asked.

It didn't sound like he wanted to laugh now. More that he was concerned and also realised the mortification level being wedged into a snappish chair had sent me to. I peeked up at him, horror-struck to see the crowd of women in my peripheral vision, all clustered on the stairs beside our seats.

*Oh. My. Goodness.*

I turned to my right, giving them a winning smile and launching into Lola mode. "Well, that was an experience!"

The women appeared relieved, and each one seemed connected to me by the threads that only females recognise when another is deeply embarrassed and does her best to hide it.

"So you wanna come learn cheerleading?" a blonde asked. "We have pom-poms for you."

I smiled in response. The women started walking down the steps, and SJ spoke to them. I couldn't hear what he was saying but turned to Blake so it didn't look like I was listening.

"I really don't want to do this," I whispered to him.

"I think we should go up into the private box now," Blake suggested.

I couldn't have agreed more and turned to find the cheerleaders were back to prancing around and SJ Stevens had joined us on the steps.

"I sent them off," he said. "Told them there's no time to teach you. Kinda thought you'd appreciate that."

I did appreciate it, and I smiled at him.

SJ returned to the court, issuing orders for everyone to get moving. They had to change into their kit and the fans would be arriving soon. I walked up the steps to the private box with Blake, never so relieved to sit in a normal seat that didn't fancy eating my bum.

A young brunette lady in a Grand Stars sweatshirt and cap poked her head around the door. "Would you like some refreshments?"

"A glass of wine, please," I said, wondering if it was a little too early to be indulging, and during a basketball game at that—one where I'd be singing.

"And you, sir?" She smiled at Blake.

"Make that a bottle of white, please," he said. Then, once she'd gone, "I think you need more than one glass, sweetheart."

"Blimey, I'm not a lush, but it'll help take the sting out of everything." I leant down to massage my thigh, which was throbbing a bit from being squashed in the evil chair.

"Hey, let me do that."

He lifted my leg onto his lap and smoothed away all the hurt. I closed my eyes, wondering where I got my clutz tendencies from—and whether I'd ever be without them.

"I hope so," I murmured, lulled towards a doze by Blake's expert hands.

"You hope what?" he asked.

"Oh, nothing..."

Just before the server came back, Blake settled my foot on the floor. I smiled as the Grand Stars Brunette carried in a tray with two glasses and a bottle of chianti on top. We thanked her and she left. Blake uncorked the wine—*me in the seat, me in the seat!*—poured then handed me a full glass.

It went down like a treat. Ah, this was the life.

**Diary**

## Girlfriend

Hmm! Somehow this fun-filled day has left me with a slight hole inside me. I couldn't help but feel a little alone. I have the perfect companion, one which I see myself going through all journeys of life with, but I couldn't help but see those cheerleaders and feel as though my life is lacking that Female Friendship. Why I can't just be satisfied with the most perfect man and friend in the world goodness only knows, but something somewhere inside me longs for that girlie companionship.

Come to think of it, other than Jenna, which I don't believe counts as she's my sister, I have no female friends. Not one! Am I a girl deflector? Maybe I'm one of those unapproachable women who give off that 'I'm a bitch don't bother trying to be my friend' vibe?

I always saw myself as a happy-go-lucky, getting-on-with-everybody kind of girl. So where are my cheerleaders? No wonder I'm so afraid to be apart from Blake. I have no one else to catch me when I'm tossed in the air by life's ups and downs. No one to meet for a good old chinwag and cup of tea to moan about coupled life and the hardship of relationships. I suppose Roo-Roo is pretty close to a female companion as they come. Although, there is a longing in me for at least one girly girlfriend.

Mission set. Find a BFF, my very own cheerleader.

# 13

The game had been exciting yesterday, as had been singing at half-time then the talks with the Grand Stars managerial team about what they expected from me as the face of their sportswear brand. Thankfully, all I had to do next time I was in New York was to have my photos taken in their snazzy clothing. I asked if I could bring my own photographer—I had Austin in mind, he made me feel relaxed—and they said sure, no problem. Okay, Austin would have to fly over from London, but I'd bet he'd love the chance to work over here. David would be arriving soon and would take care of anything else that might have come up that I wasn't aware of as yet, as well as arranging for Austin to work with me again.

After a good night's sleep, I woke to thinking my mishaps at the court had all been one of my silly dreams. If that was the way my mind wanted to play it, I wasn't about to argue. Today was more downtime—unusual for me to have so much in such a short space of time. I was usually rushed off my feet marching to the record company's drum. And to David's. Sometimes, though, it worked out that I had to work every other day, and others I had to work six days straight with no break. Blake had gone to work but said he'd be back to take me to lunch. So I had a morning to myself—with no idea how to spend it.

Once I'd showered, I made a cup of tea. It didn't taste the same as it did back home, and it brought on a pang of missing my dad. If I'd felt like this at my place I would have gone and bugged him for a while, nattering over a cuppa and catching up on what he'd been up to. It had been such a long time since I'd got together with him in person for a good old natter.

I checked the clock. It was too early in London for me to give him a call, and if Jenna was at work, coming to the end of a nightshift at the nursing home, she'd be too busy to chat. And as for Roo-Roo, he'd still be in a deep sleep. He didn't get out of bed for anyone before seven a.m.

Was this what it would be like if I lived in America full time? I'd need to make some friends so that on those rare days I wasn't working and Blake was, I could have some human interaction other than whoever was on TV.

So instead of calling the important people in my life, I fired off an email to each of them. After that it was a case of clock-watching. Bored and restless, I wandered around the penthouse. Blake's studio was one room I'd hardly ever been in. He hadn't said it was out of bounds or private, and to be honest, there hadn't really been much time for me really have a good nose and see what was in there anyway. The times I'd spent in his penthouse were mainly used for sleeping.

I entered feeling guilty, like I was invading his personal space. Ahead were drawing desks covered in plans for what looked like a house. From what I could make out it was three-storey, because instead of an attic there was a recording studio. So this was a house for a music artist, and I wondered who it was. On a pad beside the drawings, notes had been scribbled. The project was a renovation, and a to-do list had some jobs ticked off. All that appeared to be left was the small things like rubber strips around the baths and kitchen worktops.

I glanced to my left, ready to turn and leave but was stopped short by the other half of the room. A human-height canvas was held up on a huge easel, and an image of me stared back, hair a tangled mess, wild and crazy. My cheeks had faint scratches on them, and I realised Blake had depicted me on that night I'd hidden in the bush outside Gianni's restaurant. I'd felt at my most embarrassed and vulnerable there, thinking that the state of me would put him off. But he hadn't cared, and this painting proved it. A fond memory he'd perhaps created while we'd been apart, recalling my features perfectly.

I left the room, bursting with emotion. I needed to hug and squeeze him but had to be content with hugging myself. I sprawled on the sofa and stared up at the New York painting, studying every detail he'd added. His talent left me in awe—I could just about draw a stick man—and while the minutes until I saw him again dragged their tick-tock backsides, I drifted to sleep feeling warm and fuzzy inside.

Blake grinned across at me from the driver's seat.

"Come on, where are we going?" I asked. "You can't just say we're going out, that I don't need to dress up, and not at least give me some idea of the venue."

"Okay," he said. "The Hamptons. That's the venue. I was going to arrange a picnic, but the weather isn't too bright and it looks like rain's on the way."

All right, so he was making this a surprise destination. I could handle that. Except I couldn't. I'd never been very good at being kept in the dark, knowing that whoever was doing the surprise knew more than me. It made me do that scenario thing, where I dreamed up all sorts of stuff that, of course, never ended up being the surprise at all. At least I had a timeframe now, though. The Hamptons wasn't far away, just under two hours of driving, quicker if Blake put his foot down. Last time we'd been there we'd walked on the beach and I'd laughed so much my tummy hurt. Those first two weeks of our relationship were such special times, where I'd got to know Blake a little better. To be going back brought on nostalgia.

I watched the scenery roll by outside, reliving in my head the time from when we'd first met to now. So much had happened—enough to fill a decade, not just a year—and if the rest of our lives were as jam-packed, I'd go to my grave a very fulfilled woman.

We arrived at The Hamptons, and Blake turned down a few streets until we came to an elegant avenue. The trees swayed in the breeze, waving their twiggy arms as if in welcome. The avenue was quiet, with houses on gated lots, each one secure behind wrought-iron fences about eight-feet high. Decorative spikes topped each fence pole, in the shape of a spearhead.

One house dominated the row of three to our left. Huge and pure white with black trim and shutters, its simplicity made it graceful. A slate roof with arched, lead-paned windows had a fat chimney stretching up at either end. The front door was a double, the top curved like the windows, reminding me of a church back in London. The surroundings were beautifully manicured lawns with slim trees and pretty flowerbeds which hugged a pea-gravelled driveway. It was the perfect house, one I'd have chosen to live in.

Blake navigated up to the gate, opening his window to reach out and slide a credit card type key down a device attached to a slender pole. The gates yawned open, and Blake drove through, the tyres crunching over the stones.

As he eased up the drive, I watched the house come towards me, wondering if he was finally taking me to meet the rest of his family. Suddenly self-conscious because I had on jeans and a baggy sweater, and my hair was stuffed into a messy bun, I looked across at him, worried and unsure.

"It's okay," he said. "We'll be alone here."

I frowned.

"It's a work project. Something for an artist. I wanted you to see the studio, see if it has everything they'll need. I don't have a clue about these things so had to rely on the supplier's assurance that what he'd shipped was adequate."

"Um, should I be here then?" I fiddled with the strap of my handbag. "It doesn't seem right, me being at someone else's house when they're not there."

"Don't worry about it. The artist doesn't know this place is for them. The whole project is a surprise."

I felt a little bad about seeing it before they did. "Okay, so long as I'm only here to give advice."

"Not quite, but it's all good."

He parked up then got out, standing with the car door open, looking at the gardens. I joined him.

"Do you like flowers?" he asked. "I mean, does every woman want them in their garden?"

"They're pretty." I inspected the petals of a tiny rose bush. "But to be honest, I love those hedge sculpture thingies."

"Thingies?"

I nodded. "You know, where hedges are trimmed into animals or whatever."

"Oh, topiaries. Hmm. So no flowers?" He rubbed his chin.

"Not really." I reconsidered at the sight of his frown. "Maybe a rose bush or two. The climbing kind. If you look at the house from here, wouldn't it be lovely to have roses going all around that front door in an arch?"

"Hmm." He cocked his head, probably envisioning it in his mind's eye.

"Then there's plenty of petals for romantic bedroom settings. That's if the artist likes that sort of thing. You know, having petals on the bed." I blushed. Telling Blake one of my fantasies out here in the open made me feel oddly exposed, as though someone else could be listening.

"Oh, so you like that kind of thing, do you?"

"Well, not the idea of sleeping on them. Knowing my luck, I'd snore, take a deep breath, and end up with petals stuck against my nose. But seeing it all pretty, yeah. That'd be nice."

"Awesome."

I dug into him with my elbow. "So, let me see this studio, then."

He used the card to gain access to the house, and an alarm buzzed then erupted into a duel-toned screech. The foyer was large and empty, the sound bouncing off the floor and seriously high walls.

I stepped inside once he'd shut the racket off, turning in circles on the harlequin tiles and gasping at the wide staircase ahead. It belonged in one of those black-and-white films, a Scarlett O'Hara jobby, and I could just see myself sweeping down the steps of a morning, long kimono flowing behind me.

"Oh! It's beautiful."

He smiled. "Isn't it? The whole place is. Just needs a lot of furniture. Come and see."

He led me through the rooms, each one more elaborate than those before with their grand chandeliers and fireplaces big enough to stand up in. This really was a palace fit for a princess.

The polished wooden floors shone in shafts of sunlight that streaked through the windows, shadows of the lead panes making diamond patterns there. Upstairs, the largest bedroom housed a bed so vast I guessed four people could lay side by side on it. There wasn't any bedding, but I imagined a big puffy duvet that begged to be jumped on.

The main bathroom was massive, a claw-foot, black marble tub standing in the centre, large enough for two. A shower cubicle spanned one corner, the door curved, the glass embedded with what looked like scattered crystals. Gold taps on the sink were swan's heads, the water coming out of their beaks. It really was amazing.

"Bloody hell," I breathed. "I knew people lived like this but..."

"Yes, a place like this can really leave you speechless. You should have seen it a month or so ago before my men got their hands on it. The poor thing was a mess."

"But it's so beautiful now." I suddenly wanted a long, hot soak in that bath.

Blake gazed at me. "Oh yes. Beautiful."

I smiled, and he winked, walking from the room. I followed him to a staircase tucked away at the end of the landing, similar to something servants would have used in days gone by. He went up, the narrow space making him seem so broad, then disappeared around a bend. I trailed him, gripping the ornate handrail until I reached the top.

The studio was right there, no door, spread out to span maybe half the roof space. The rafters were exposed, gorgeous and shiny oak, the ceiling in between navy blue with splashes of stars painted on it.

"Oh! It would be like singing at night in here. Outside."

"Indeed."

I would love that. The times I'd busked on the streets close to midnight so I could catch the generous drunks as they'd poured out of pubs and dropped their loose change into my beret on the pavement. "These stars are such a lovely idea."

Blake let out a long breath. "Glad I got that right. So, what I want you to look at is over there."

He walked to a window in the wall, and a familiar feeling exploded in my belly. Behind that glass was a microphone and I itched to sing.

"Can I?"

He nodded, and I went inside the room. I tapped the microphone to check it was on then let the melody of one of my songs weave through my head. The words poured out of me, and I closed my eyes, feeling, as I always did, that this was what I'd been born to do. The music in my mind pitched and swelled, ebbed and flowed, and I put my heart and soul into singing just for Blake. A rush of euphoria rippled through me as I reached a crescendo and dragged the note out for as long as I could.

Song over, I opened my eyes to find him looking at me through the glass as though I was some kind of miracle.

"Wow," he said. "Just…wow."

I walked back into the main studio and rushed up to him for a cuddle, so glad he'd liked my singing.

"That's the first time you've given me a private performance," he said into my ear.

And I realised it was. "Well, I'll sing all day when we're at home if that's what floats your boat."

"It does. You've got the voice of an angel. And, before the day gets away from us, angels need lunch."

We returned downstairs, going into the back garden. A summerhouse stood at the bottom, as big as a small cottage, and inside a table had been set up with plates, glasses and cutlery.

"We can't eat here, surely," I whispered, glancing through the glass in the door as though we'd be spotted by a lurking gardener or something.

"Yes, we can. Please be seated, modom," he said in an over-the-top British accent.

I giggled and relaxed a bit. "You're still awful at the accent. You need to practise more."

I took my place at the table, peering across at a sideboard with a silver food-warmer system on top. He played server, dishing up a similar meal to the one that had been interrupted on our first dinner date at Gianni's, and I could have cried at his thoughtfulness. He must have had someone set this up while we'd been travelling.

We spent the rest of the day in the summerhouse, lounging on a comfy sofa, talking in between light naps. He jumped up at one point, as though he'd forgotten something, then nipped out, vanishing into the main house. I assumed he had to make a phone call so took the time to shake myself more awake, lethargy heavy in my bones.

He returned, looking as though he'd done something naughty. "I just had a thought."

"What kind of thought?"

"I haven't shown you what else needs doing here."

He tugged me from the sofa and led me outside, around the back of the summerhouse. It was almost dark now, a few stars struggling to shine brightly, the moon smothered in clouds. In the murk I managed to make out an expanse of concrete sitting beside a huge rectangular hole, all of it secluded beneath overhanging tree branches that almost touched the ground, creating walls of leafy curtains.

"A pool's going in there," he said and pointed at the hole. "What do you think, open air or inside?"

"Definitely inside."

"That's what I thought. There'll be a Perspex walkway from the house to here, so yes, I think you're right. Inside."

He was animated, and his dedication to his job, his passion for it, showed me another side to him.

"What about that concrete there?" I moved to stand on top of it.

It was dusty, as though sand had been sprinkled on it, and some puffed up and landed on my shoes.

"A hot tub base." He winked. "Nice place to relax and…"

"Hmm." I pursed my lips, knowing what he was thinking.

"Take your woman."

He rugby tackled me, guiding us down onto the cement. I squealed at how hard it was, and he kissed me until I had to pull away to breathe.

"There's no place I'd rather be," he said.

"What, on a cold concrete slab?"

"No, with you—anywhere with you."

I smiled and stared into his eyes. "We're here for each other, aren't we?"

"We are. Supporting the other's dreams and careers. Good times and bad."

"Seal that with another kiss?" I asked, brushing a bit of his hair out of his eyes.

"I'll seal it with more than that."

And he did, right there in the garden beneath the starry sky, the concrete our bed, the air our blankets, and the trees our curtains. Afterwards, out of breath and half dressed, we giggled and sorted out our clothing, standing to kiss again and again, with me imagining we were standing in the hot tub that had yet to be built.

"We should go." He wrapped his arms around me. "It's getting cold."

With our pleasant outing at an end, Blake escorted me back to the car. I opened my door, the interior light a bright splash in the darkness. And on my seat were rose petals from the little bush, pink and red and pretty.

It took all my strength not to stand there and cry.

# 14

Next morning, I woke to a kiss on my cheek and, as a result, butterflies doing their mental dance in my belly. I'd swear they listened to rave music. I turned my head to find Blake on his side, propping himself up on one elbow and looking at me. What a great sight to see first thing in the morning. I smiled, stretched, then cuddled into him. He was sleep-warm, his muscles relaxed, my great big personal teddy bear.

"I'm taking another day off," he said, stroking my hair. "I can't get enough of being with you."

I smiled again. I couldn't get enough of being with him either.

"So I'm going to take a quick shower then go out and get breakfast," he said. "We can eat it in bed before we have to go to Merriweather's."

Merriweather's was a big store on Fifth Avenue. I was due there at about midday to launch my new perfume, which David had arranged for me to make last year. I'd chosen the scents myself and had had much fun in the creation process.

"That sounds good." I pressed myself closer to him, reluctant to let him go. I'd give anything to stay in bed with him all day but duty called.

He kissed the top of my head.

"So, you stay there, all nice and warm, and I'll be back before you know it."

He got out of bed, and I allowed myself the luxury of watching him stride across the bedroom to the en suite. He left the door open, and I continued to stare as he got into the shower. Unfortunately, steam clouded the screen and all I was left with was a blurry, flesh-coloured image of him soaping his body. The scent of his shower gel floated into the bedroom, and I closed my eyes, pretending he was in bed with me again.

While he finished up, I listened to the sounds he made—the short squirt of deodorant, the opening of drawers, the tiny squeak of his wardrobe door being closed. All of it was familiar to me now, and it was as though I belonged here with him. And, just like when I'd stayed here before, London ceased to exist.

So my silly behaviour about moving to America had been just that—silly. I could do this. I could live wherever, so long as I was with him.

I opened my eyes as he came over to pop a kiss on my forehead. His red polo top suited him, and those jeans.

"Won't be long," he whispered then left the room.

The click of the front door closing meant I had nothing to do but wait. I snuggled beneath the covers, tucking the duvet around me so I was wedged inside a cocoon of softness. I began drifting back to sleep, a light doze where I was alert yet not far from going right under. To keep myself from falling, I pictured Blake bringing back a big McDonald's breakfast, extra sausage, and one of their large coffees. Knowing him, it was more likely to be continental, all croissants and pastries, but a girl could dream.

The front door being opened again gave me a jolt of surprise. I glanced at the clock on the bedside table. Only four minutes or so had passed since Blake had left. Had he forgotten his wallet or something? I stayed where I was for a moment, waiting for him to come into the bedroom and collect whatever it was he needed.

He never breezed in.

Footsteps tapped on the wooden flooring, but they didn't seem to be coming my way. From what I could gather, they were heading for Blake's office, or even the kitchen beside it, I couldn't be too sure. I was tempted to call out his name but a tiny voice inside me said not to. Blake's cleaner wasn't due, he'd told me he'd given her some time off, so who else would have access to his penthouse?

*Oh, what if…? What if it's a bloody burglar? What if someone saw him go out and assumed the place was empty?*

I jumped out of bed then, my mind on fire with wicked, frightening scenarios that would give any horror writer a run for their money. My imagination of old came hurtling back, where I entertained ideas of killers and nasty men who might want to abduct me. A part of me knew I was being irrational, but the fear of what people could be like beneath their surfaces had always been something I'd thought about.

With my heart throbbing like a stubbed toe, I snatched some clothes from the wardrobe and flung them on – one of Blake's T-shirts and a pair of my pyjama bottoms. If I was going to be confronted by a marauder, I'd be doing it clothed, not naked. There was no way I was letting some stranger see my private bits.

I tiptoed over to the door, holding my breath and feeling ridiculous that I was acting this way. Honestly, it had to be Blake or the cleaner, didn't it? Maybe she'd forgotten she'd been given time off. Or something? Perhaps?

*Like she'd forget she had time off. It's Blake, it has to be.*

With a bit more confidence, I peered through the bedroom doorway into the large lounge. All appeared in order there, although it was a tad dark as the blinds hadn't been opened yet. I looked over at the two doors to my left. The kitchen one was wide open, the room in darkness, but the office one was ajar. Creamy light spilt out as a rectangle in the gloom, a strip slashing across the floor where the door usually met the jamb. The *tap-tap-tap* of the keyboard being used barked out into the quiet.

So Blake had gone into his office, then.

*Maybe he got a call and he's had to come back to check on something for someone at work.*

Telling myself it really could only be him, I padded over to the door. The odour of a cologne I'd smelt somewhere before tickled my nose, and my stomach rolled over then tightened. Where did I recognise it from? I racked my brains trying to figure it out, all the while knowing, with a heavy dread seeping into me, that it *wasn't* Blake in that room.

In my panic, I'd left my phone on the bedside table.

*Shall I go and get it? Oh, bloody hell, I don't know what to do!*

I pressed my back to the wall and sidled along so I could peek through the gap by the hinges. I got a narrow view of Blake's desk—just his monitor, which was on and displaying some text or other—and the tall Tiffany table lamp behind it. Shuffling sounds startled me some more, scattering my nerves so that goosebumps popped up on my arms. I stopped myself from gasping. Held my breath. With my pulse thudding in my ears, I shifted in an attempt to see more of the room.

An elbow came into view.

An elbow covered in a grey suit sleeve.

*Blake has a red polo top on…*

The arm extended, the person reaching out to jab at the keyboard again. A smattering of hairs on the back of the hand caught the light from the lamp, sparking recognition in my mind.

*Ginger. What's he doing here?*

Was it normal for him to just come into Blake's home like this? And what was the normal thing for me to do now? Go in and say hi?

I let out the breath I'd been holding and it sounded way too loud.

Ginger moved across a few inches, enabling me to see the back of him properly. He looked about furtively, as though he sensed he was being watched. I stopped breathing again, my lungs burning—I hadn't had a chance to suck in more air. My face grew hot, and I stared, wide-eyed, in case he turned and caught me spying. He tilted his head, and I guessed he was listening intently.

He started tapping the keyboard again, bending over to study the screen. This seemed dodgy to me, his whole demeanour that of someone who was somewhere he shouldn't be. I breathed again, trying not to gasp, my head light from lack of air. I held my hand to my chest, the thud of my heart pounding against my palm. This wasn't how I'd envisaged spending my morning, sneaking up on a man, being scared witless because there really was something off about this—off about him.

It didn't feel right at all.

Blake must have told him to come here, to access a work file or whatever. I couldn't see his brother from another mother just entering his house whenever he felt like it. Then again, Jenna had a key to my place.

*But she never goes in unless I say it's okay after she's checked with me first.*

I wanted to clear my throat then go into the office, find out what he was doing, but I remained stuck in place. His threat in Gianni's bounced around in my head. The jarring, alien ring of a phone nearly had me jumping out of my skin and screeching. I managed to keep quiet and still, knowing it must be Ginger's mobile—none of the phones here went off like that.

He fished into his pocket and answered the call, mobile pressed to his face. Was he shaking? If he was meant to be here, that kind of reaction didn't make sense.

"Hello?" he said.

For a second I forgot he was on the phone and nearly answered him.

*Concentrate! This isn't a time for messing up.*

"Um, yeah. I could swing by your place in about an hour. I'm in the office at the moment. What? No, the business office."

*Oh, you little liar…*

A memory from one of my other times here came slamming back into my mind. Funny enough, I'd been spying on Ginger then too, except Blake had been with him. Ginger had gone on about people lying, as though he was virtuous and would never dream of doing such a thing. Yet here he was, telling porkies to whoever was on the phone.

"You're what?" he said loudly. "Oh, right. A day off. Again." He shook his head, prodding at the keyboard once more. "Well, that's none of my business. What are your plans then?" He paused in typing. Snapped his head up. "Err, lovely. That's just awesome."

*Is it me, or did he sound panicked then? And him mentioning a day off. Is he talking to Blake? If he is, he's told him he's at the business office, so if he's allowed to just breeze in here whenever the fancy takes him, why lie about where he is?*

He did something with the mouse that made the document on screen disappear. Then he darted his head left to right, as if checking out the stuff on top of the desk.

"So where's Charlotte, then?" Silence. "At *your place*?" He jammed one hand into his hair and his breathing grew heavy. "Well, I have to get going. Some of us have work to do." His laughter was false, forced but quiet. "Yeah, yeah, whatever."

He shoved his phone into his pocket, and before I got caught, I rushed back through the lounge, imagining him coming out of the office and catching me as I rounded the bedroom doorjamb. I hurled myself into bed, yanking the covers right up to my chin in case he came in to check on me.

I couldn't get my breathing under control. It wouldn't behave itself, coming out all ragged and noisy. I blew out through pursed lips then inhaled deeply, willing myself to calm down. I screwed my eyes tightly shut then relaxed the lids, making out I was asleep.

Footsteps clacked on the lounge floor, fast and with purpose.

*Please, just leave. Don't come in here…*

Connor was coming this way, I knew it. The footsteps were getting louder by the millisecond. Then they stopped. Was he in the doorway? I sensed him there, staring at me, and thank goodness I was breathing almost normally. I did a fake asleep-stretch, hoping he'd think I was about to wake up any moment.

"Shit," he whispered.

*Shit, indeed. You're up to something, you naughty little man.*

The smack of his shoes on the floor told me he was running out of the penthouse. The front door closed quietly, and I waited for a while before I opened my eyes. Then I got out of bed, deciding that if he'd tricked me and was still in the lounge, I'd make out I'd just got up and that it was completely natural to find him there.

He wasn't there.

I strode to the office, going straight to the computer. The monitor had gone into autosave mode, so I wiggled the mouse, bringing the screen back to life. There was nothing but a screensaver and a few files on the desktop. But three minimised documents caught my eye, their tabs sitting innocently on the bottom taskbar. I brought one up to fill the monitor. It was some kind of accounting software, column after column of figures filling it. Curious, I enlarged one of the other windows. It was for a bank, showing that if Ginger had accessed it, he'd signed out. The third was yet another bank. I shrugged it off, thinking that if Ginger hadn't properly closed these windows, he must be allowed to access things like this on Blake's computer. Otherwise, why would he leave them there if he had something to hide?

Unless he only *thought* he'd closed them down properly? What if, in his rush and panic, he'd forgotten to double-check?

Then another niggle of doubt crept in.

If he was allowed in here and wasn't up to anything bad, he wouldn't need to fib about *being* in here.

My crazy brain went into overdrive, throwing out reason after reason as to why this situation didn't feel right. Should I tell Blake? Was it any of my business that his brother had been here? The fact that he'd been so jittery was the only thing making me think deceptive shenanigans were afoot. And he'd come to the bedroom door—to make sure I was asleep and hadn't been aware of him?

I stared at the screen, nauseated and confused as to what to do.

The front door opening again had me shrieking this time. I dashed out into the lounge, ready to give Ginger what for, but Blake stood there holding a McDonald's bag, a big smile on his face.

He held the bag up and shook it. "You're meant to be in bed for breakfast, remember?"

I smiled, so relieved it was him, and because he looked so happy, I decided to leave off telling him what I'd seen until tonight. It would give me some time to process things and work out the best way to approach the subject.

Gawd, who did I think I was, Detective Inspector Taylor?

# 15

The breakfast sat heavy in my belly, a big fat wedge of weight that I wished I hadn't eaten. I was sure I'd have enjoyed it more if it hadn't been for the latest Ginger saga playing on my mind. Still, it was probably nothing, so I focused on soaking up my surroundings.

I was standing on Fifth Avenue in my skinny jeans, a fitted white blouse, a trendy black biker's leather jacket and a dainty little patterned chiffon scarf. Oh my word. All my life I'd barely allowed myself to dream about shopping in Merriweather's, let alone having my own product in those perfect little Merriweather's bags!

I was merrier than the shop name and felt like a superstar. Local and UK press had gathered – I recognised some of the paps from London. It would never cease to amaze me that they followed me wherever I went. And to just take pictures of me going inside a shop? It was crazy. I knew I was famous, but somehow that knowledge still hadn't fully sunk in. I took it as a good sign that my launch of a fragrance was much anticipated if it was deemed newsworthy.

A long queue snaked alongside the building. Were they all here to purchase my perfume? The shop was already open, so I could only assume there would be a separate area for the yummy-smelling goods. The weather wasn't too great, and many of the customers had thick jackets on. Some even wore beanie hats.

Blake squeezed my hand. "They're all here for you, Herman," he whispered.

I smiled up at him, conscious of the photographers taking pictures. A tap on my shoulder had me spinning around, daftly thinking it was Ginger. It wasn't. David stood there, his attention on the queue.

"I knew it." He nodded and looked at me. "Am I on the ball or what?"

I laughed. Yeah, I had to give him credit. He knew exactly what to do and where to steer my career.

"Morning, by the way. I arrived late last night." He tipped his head at Blake. "So, are you ready then?" he asked me.

"As I'll ever be."

Blake and I followed David into the shop amid much cheering and clapping from those in the queue. I wanted to stuff my knuckles in my mouth once we were inside. The shop was huge, and oh, la-di-dah, so very posh. I couldn't believe I was here and that I'd be signing perfume boxes with silver Sharpies for the best part of the day.

*Hashtag Living the Dream.*

I gazed at the large table to the right that held box after box of my perfume, Daydreamer. I felt like squealing in excitement upon seeing the pretty packaging, sparkly and candy pink, the letters cerise with silver glitter mixed in. A couple of sales assistants stood behind the table, looking gorgeous in their Merriweather's uniforms, and they wore badges—badges!—with the word Daydreamer streaking across the middle.

I was daydreaming now, wasn't I? I had to be. This was all too much to take in. I waited for David to talk to what must have been the manager, who pointed to the door we'd just come through with a look of concern on his face.

"Oh, *him,*" David said. "Yes, yes, he's our man."

I had no idea what they were talking about so kept an eye on the manager as he strutted to the door then went outside. I glanced over at David, who mouthed "Photographer" and gave me a huge smile. I experienced the usual flutter of nerves at knowing David had obviously arranged for a proper photo shoot here.

With no time to wind myself up about it, I was swept away from Blake and taken behind the table to stand between the two assistants. I gave him a quick smile to apologise for being snatched away, and he smiled back then winked, letting me know he understood. I wondered how he felt about seeing his girlfriend in this capacity instead of in his penthouse or my place doing normal, everyday things. I had nothing to compare it to as I'd yet to see him working.

I said hello to the assistants, who stared at me as if they were star-struck, so I held their hands, wanting to make it a little more relaxed for them. A commotion at the door had my attention taken from them, though, and I stared over that way to see what was going on.

The photographer had his back to me. He was wedged in the doorway, his camera and tripod half in, half out of the shop, and it looked as though no one had thought to help him carry his things inside. The heavy door pressed on his backside, effectively pinning him against the jamb. My instinct was to rush over there and help him out—he must have been so embarrassed—but David got there first, bless him. He pulled the door wide then leant round the photographer and said something. The photographer nodded then shuffled inside, grappling with his equipment like a nervous nelly.

He turned to face the shop, blinking behind thick-lens glasses, his teeth hanging out to dry, the whiteness of his ruffle-fronted shirt glaring beneath the lights.

*Oh my, it's Austin Powers...*

I didn't know his real name—Austin was the one I'd secretly given him last time he'd taken pictures of me for my first album cover—and I quickly glanced at Blake to check his reaction. Blake had kind of met Austin last year in a restaurant when he hadn't known I was famous. At least this time I didn't have to worry about my secret getting out. Everything was in the open.

Blake grinned.

"*Lowwlah*!" Austin screeched, waltzing towards me as best he could with his bag and tripod constantly battering his leg.

He plonked his things on the floor then lurched forwards, stretching his arms out for a hug. I let go of the assistants' hands and indulged him, smiling and laughing, relieved it was him who'd be taking my pictures. He was such an odd duck but cute with it, and always made me feel relaxed. That he resembled, spoke and acted like Austin Powers only endeared him to me more.

He kissed my cheek then eased back, holding the tops of my arms as though I was a long-lost friend. He displayed his awesome teeth in an incredibly wide grin. "Oh, it's so good to see you, baby, yeah! And in New York again, no less." He giggled, rolling his eyes and shaking his head, hair bouncing all over the place. "I haven't been back to London since the last time I saw you here." His eyes twinkled. "Found myself a little love interest the same as you did." He winked, resting his top teeth over his lower lip. "What do you think about that, *Lowwlah*?"

"That's wonderful," I said, genuinely pleased for him.

"Now then, David wants me to take a few images of you posing with the perfume, so while I get myself sorted, you get hold of the biggest bottle possible, yeah?"

Before I could answer, he picked up his belongings and tottered away on his block heels, legs as slim as liquorice in his black skinny-fit trousers. He was wearing a blue velvet suit jacket with black lapels, the back hem caught inside his waistband, and it seemed he didn't care one bit. He swivelled to face me, winking and nodding exaggeratedly while he set up his tripod.

*Oh my word, this is going to be fun.*

One of the assistants handed me a large bottle of Daydreamer. I underestimated the weight and almost dropped it. After taking the lid off, I brought the bottle to my nose and sniffed. The familiar scent took me right back to when I'd first created the scent, long before I'd met Blake. I'd got lucky with a perfumery that had wanted a celebrity to market. David knew so many people, and although I wasn't exactly a big star then, they'd wanted me on their team. If someone had told me back then that the man of my dreams would accompany me at the launch, I would have thought they were mad.

"Right then, *Lowwlah,*" Austin said, opening his flash umbrella. "Almost ready. If you want to have a few practice runs at spraying perfume on yourself, you do that, darling."

I balanced the bottle on my palm, gripping the base tight so I didn't drop it. I looked down to touch the nozzle. My finger slipped, pressing it, and I waited for the spray to land delicately on my throat.

It landed on my face. Right in my bloody eyes.

"Argh!" I bellowed and dropped the bottle to lift my hands to my face. I scrunched my eyes up, hearing a thud then the tinkle of broken glass, and staggered around blindly. I waved my arms about, my hand smacking what must have been one of the assistants.

"Ow!" she said.

I pictured her clutching the struck body part in agony. "Oh my goodness, I'm *so* sorry," I choked out. Scent fumes exploded in my mouth and down my throat. My backside crashed into the table and, with eyes watering like sprinklers switched on at full blast, I struggled to keep upright. "Really, so, so sorry!"

Careening here, there and everywhere, I managed to prise my soaked eyes open, peering through what felt like enormous, puffy slits. I faced the door, and to my mortification, some people in the queue outside were rubbernecking at the window, watching me make a complete spectacle of myself. I groaned, whipping around so my back was to as many people as possible.

A tissue was handed to me over my shoulder.

"Thanks," I said, unable to speak louder than a whisper. My throat was dry, and it didn't help that the contents of the broken bottle of perfume had decided to suffocate me.

"Someone clean up that mess," David ordered. "Are you okay?" he asked me. "Do you need some time out?" He placed his hand on my shoulder and squeezed.

Touched by his concern, I shook my head and dabbed at my eyes, wishing, not for the first time in my career, that the ground would swallow me up. It had never listened to me when I'd asked it to help me out in the past and I didn't expect it to now. As always, I'd have to blunder through another of my mishaps, laughing and joking, telling everyone I was so clumsy and apologising far too much.

I turned to do just that, sticking to the same old routine and explaining I'd always been accident prone so they didn't need to worry about me. Blake stared in shock, concern clear on his face, and I shook my head a little so he didn't feel he had to come over and help out. Austin watched, his teeth resembling a rabbit's, lips pursed around the front two, and I found it in me to giggle and see the funny side of things. I glanced left then right to check on the battered assistant, but she wasn't there and I could only imagine she'd scampered off, wounded and embarrassed—and all because of me.

"The other lady?" I said to the remaining assistant. "Is she okay?"

"Oh, yes. You just poked her in the eye a bit, that's all."

*Poked her in the eye a bit? That's all?*

Oh my bloody goodness, I felt so sorry for her that I wanted to find her and make everything all right again. That wasn't possible, though. David was asking for one of the makeup ladies in another department to come along and fix my face, and the assistant was valiantly trying to help me mop up my cheeks.

"Thank you," I said to her. "If I don't see your friend before I go, would you please tell her I'm really sorry?"

"Oh, no worries." She smiled and scrunched up her shoulders so her earlobes rested on them. "She'll be so pleased you poked her like that. I mean, when she walked off wiping her face with a tissue, some tears came off onto it. You can bet she'll frame it—she's a real fan."

I knew that was supposed to make me feel better, but it only served to heap more guilt onto the already gigantic pile thumping around inside me.

"I'll sign a perfume box for her," I said, forcing a smile. "Would you make sure she gets it?"

"Of course!"

With that sorted, I allowed a pretty little lady to retouch my makeup.

"There," she said. "No one would even know you'd had mascara streaks all over your face."

*Thank goodness Austin didn't take any pictures of me like that!*

I took a deep breath and risked looking at David, who was coming around to my side of the table.

"Only Lola could do something so amusing," he said from the side of his mouth. "Woman, there's never a dull moment with you around. I *love* working with you, do you know that?" He lightly mock-punched my arm. "So go and get 'em, Miss Lola. Do your thing."

He walked away, and relief scoffed the guilt. Putting on my professional head, I dropped the tissue out of sight and slapped on a smile. David was such a darling, having faith in me the way he did.

"There we go, *Lowwlah*!" Austin hollered, positioning his camera up by his eye. "You know how it's done. That's it. Smile for me. Pose for the camera, baby, yeah!" He took picture after picture, walking back and forth in front of me. "Show me that perfume bottle, sweetcheeks. Hold it right up!"

I obeyed, grinning hard, shoving all thoughts of the mishap from my mind. With enthusiastic encouragement from Austin, I did my 'thing', pleased that Blake and David watched me from near the doors, both smiling, both looking as though they were proud of me. Then I decided to go outside and sing for the crowd, my voice strong and sure.

Some days were just *so* good. I returned inside the shop, thankful that the spilled perfume and broken bottle had been cleared up. The crowd came in and people jostled one another to get to the table first. The word 'good' didn't even cover it.

This part of the day, as Blake would say, was awesome.

# 16

I was worried. A day that had started out weirdly, then switched to awesome, might well switch yet again. Once we'd arrived back at Blake's penthouse and had eaten, settling down in front of the TV, the return of the early morning's event sneaked into my mind.

*Ginger.*

"Conner dropped by this morning," I said as I stroked Blake's bare arm with my fingertips.

"He did? Cool. Did you say hi? Is that why you were up and about when I got home?" Blake tucked his arm behind my back and hugged me closer.

I took a couple of seconds to bask in his comforting hug then pushed on. "Yes, he woke me by going into your office. I thought you'd returned, that you'd forgotten something."

"Ah, he comes in here every so often. Obviously has a key—I gave it to him. Sometimes I do work from home and forget to upload it into our communal system. He might have needed a document or whatever."

That made sense. But I wasn't sure I fancied Ginger stopping by while I was here—not unless he knocked first anyway. I could be in the shower or anything, and he could come in and stare at me and I wouldn't know anything about it if shampoo had gone into my eyes.

*Ugh. No. Don't think about that.*

I had to say something. "Um, is it possible for him to knock first while I'm staying here?"

A slight frown from Blake had me realising I'd maybe overstepped the mark. They were brothers, and who was I to come along and stop any previous arrangements? Still, I wasn't comfortable with it, and surely Blake would understand why.

"Don't get me wrong," I babbled, wanting that frown of his to go away, "he's entitled to come here whenever he wants—it's your home and he's your brother—but sometimes I kind of...um...walk about naked after a shower, you know that, before I get dressed, to dry myself off, to get a bit of air to my skin"—*stop waffling*—"and if he came in and I didn't hear him, he might get an eyeful of something he wasn't expecting, and I'd get freaked out finding him there and"—*tell him what you remember from when you first met Ginger*—"if you recall, in Gianni's restaurant, there was tension because Ging, um, Connor tends to like your girlfriends or something? I can't remember what it was exactly, but that's always stuck with me and I'd hate for him to see me with no clothes on and—"

"Okay, take a breath."

I did, a great big lungful of it. My mouth had run away with me in that attempt to stop the ridges of Blake's frown getting any deeper, but at least I'd got it all off my chest.

*Not all of it. You've got to tell him what Ginger said in Gianni's and also what you saw on that computer.*

My stomach rolled over at the prospect.

"I understand," Blake said. He smiled. "I'd feel the same if Jenna just waltzed into your place while I was there, so yeah, I'll tell him to knock next time and to only come in if he gets no answer."

That could still be tricky. "But what if I was in the shower and didn't hear him knock?"

"Ah. Right." He rubbed the side of one finger over his bottom lip. "Okay. I'll fix it. I get what you're saying."

I was glad he did and could only hope he got what I had to say next. I didn't fancy another spat—they were so bloody awful—but if I didn't tell him I'd burst.

"Thanks." I waited a beat, getting the words straight in my head before I blurted them out. Blurting wasn't wise here. I had to think properly and say what I had to say in a calm manner. "Does he usually access bank accounts and things from your computer, then?"

"Say what?"

That had got his attention. He sat bolt upright, drawing his arm out from behind my back, then leant forwards to reach for his glass.

Oh no. That brought on memories of our last serious 'discussion' and a blob of unease began mooching through my tummy. He drank some wine—sipping, thank goodness—and stared towards the front door.

"Not that I recall," he said.

I sat quietly, although I wanted to say something about the document with the numbers and columns on it. But I had a better idea. "I left the documents he had up on the screen. I wasn't sure if I should close them down or whether you'd let him know while you were on the phone with him this morning to leave them there."

"On the phone?" His frown was back full force.

"Um, yes. I gathered it was you on the phone with him because he mentioned a day off—and you were having a day off. And he asked where I was."

"The little…" Blake swallowed more wine. A lot of it. "He said he was in the main office when I called."

He'd spoken more to himself than to me, and I'd swear I could see the cogs in his brain working overtime. What with Blake's thoughts about Ginger and the scaffolding incident, I imagined his mind was spinning now. I hated the fact that I'd given him reason to doubt his brother again, but what else could I do? I loved Blake and if Ginger was up to no good—which I really thought he was now—Blake had a right to know.

He got up. "I'm just going to check those web pages a second." Striding to the steps that led to the upper lounge floor, he said over his shoulder, "I bet it's nothing, but it's best to take a look, right?"

He was trying to convince himself, I knew that, and I felt all kinds of horrible watching him walk away. If someone told me the same story about Jenna, would I believe she'd been doing something underhand?

*No way – because she's never done an underhand thing in her life. Ginger is just…shifty.*

Blake went into the office, and I waited for a moment with my breath held. I so wanted this to be nothing, something I'd suspected that could be easily explained. Blake's silence and the length of time he'd been in his office worried me, though, so I got up and joined him at his desk. He was rubbing his mouth with his finger again, his eyes narrowed, and he stared at two windows that he'd brought up side by side. They were to do with the banks.

"Is everything okay?" I asked.

He jumped, as though he'd been in such deep thought he hadn't heard me come in. I rested my hand on his shoulder—I didn't know what else to do.

"Uh, yeah. It's just the work bank and...Connor's," he said. "I'm sure he was just checking the finances. There's the accounting document there as well, you see that? And as for the other bank, well, that's his. Maybe he had to pay some bills or he needed to check his balance or... Whatever, it's fine."

For the most part, Blake usually said things precisely, his sentences measured. Just now he'd sounded more like me, rushing to make excuses, pushing the words out too quickly. I rubbed his back, wanting to comfort him, wanting his explanation to be the right one. But I didn't believe it was. Ginger was up to something, I knew it.

"Yes, that's probably it," I offered, my way of sitting on the fence.

For now.

Blake turned to look at me. The mechanism in his chair squeaked, giving me a mini jolt. I was on edge and needed to remain impartial so we didn't go down Argue Avenue.

"Are you okay about Connor?" He took my free hand and made circles on the back of it with his thumb. "I'm close to him, but not as close as I am to my sister. If him coming in here bothers you, that's fine, but I'm worried that if you're a little jealous of him…" He laughed nervously. "You did tell me to give it to you straight in future… I'm worried how you'll react to my sister. Because she's…very different to Connor. Like I told you before, she'll come across as super in your face at times and…"

*Like Ginger doesn't?*

I waited for what Blake would say next but he didn't say a thing.

"Jealous? Of him?" I laughed too. "Er, no. All I was worried about was that he was doing something he shouldn't be. That's the end of it. If you're happy with what you see here, then that's that."

I really, *really* didn't want to argue with him. We'd got ourselves balanced again and rocking the boat now would just be silly. I'd keep any opinions I had about Ginger to myself—unless I had proof he was up to no good. If I managed to see him without Blake around, I'd maybe ask him what he'd been doing, but at the moment, for tonight, I had to let it go.

Tomorrow and the days after, though, were a different matter. Now that the thought had come into my mind, confronting him seemed more and more appealing. I knew myself well enough that if I didn't at least bring the subject up with Ginger so I could see his reaction, this situation would eat away at me. Why would he need the business bank, his personal bank, and the accounting document up all at once? I might have been naïve in some respects, but this just stank of Eau de Bullshit.

"Listen, what if I set up a coffee date for you and him?" Blake suggested. "Then you can have a bonding session."

Oh, the perfect opportunity had been plonked right into my lap. "Coffee would be great. I could do with getting to know him, plus it'll give you a couple of hours to get some work done. I know you're itching to get back to it."

Blake grinned.

*Crisis averted, phew! High-five to me!*

He called Ginger and set up a date for about ten tomorrow morning. I was to meet him at his apartment then we'd go to a coffee shop nearby. That was fine by me. The sooner I got this stuff out of my head the better.

We left our conversation at that, returning to the sofa to finish watching the film, although Blake didn't look as interested in it as he had been before I'd brought up the subject of Ginger. An hour or so later, swaddled beside him in bed, with Blake's gentle breathing telling me he'd drifted off, I tried to get to sleep myself. Of course, reaching the Land of Nod wasn't easy sometimes, not while I had things on my mind. I argued with myself, working hard to put things into perspective. I wanted so badly to learn how to see the other side of the coin, to grow and mature in any situation.

After an hour or so had passed, there was nothing left for me to do but turn to my trusty diary. Things always seemed better once I'd had a good old rant in there. I hoped tonight wouldn't be the exception.

**Diary**

**Ranty McPanty**

The Ginger situation is bothering me more and more. I'd usually ignore these feelings as me just having a huge imagination, but this time it feels like gut instinct. Okay, that isn't always what it seems and I've been wrong in the past when I've followed my intuition, but I feel so strongly about this that I…

Oh. Just say it outright and be done with it.

Something doesn't add up and I can't ignore it. It wouldn't be right!

Okay, now that's out of the way, I'm going to make a firm decision. When I have coffee with Ginger in the morning, I'm definitely going to confront him. Hear it straight from the horse's mouth, see what his excuse is.

And here's something else that's been going through my mind. I hate thinking badly of Blake, but I really think the fact that they grew up together may be clouding his judgement. No one wants to find out their family member isn't who they thought, I know that, but Ginger's Blake's accountant, for goodness sake. He could be up to anything. And that scaffolding business, his threat to me—that's just plain scary.

But he could be up to nothing. Accountants work with banks, don't they?

Argh! This is doing my head in.

Should I risk upsetting Ginger, which, in turn, might make Blake extremely angry? Or should I just ignore my strong feeling that something may be happening?

No. I've already said I've made a firm decision and I'm sticking to it.

I'll speak to that ginger creep about it tomorrow.

There. Sorted. Now I need to get some sleep.

# 17

Armed with Ginger's address, I set off down the street, glad I'd opted to walk rather than have Blake drop me off in his car. Ginger only lived a block away, and I was sure I could manage well enough by myself. Anyway, the time alone would do me good. I planned to use it to think about how I was going to broach the subject with him. Blurting out, 'Hey, Connor, are you fiddling your brother's accounts by any chance?' wasn't the ideal way to go.

I felt incredibly like a wise old detective, except I wasn't elderly and wore a huge pair of sunglasses to somewhat hide my identity, a comfy pair of jeans and a thick sweatshirt instead of a twin set and pearls. I marched along, determined to get to the bottom of this. One way or another, things were going to be resolved today and I could get back to the important task of working.

I passed the coffee shop where we were supposed to be going. People filled all the available seats, and the fact that it was super busy gave me reason to pause and stare through the window. My initial thought of confronting him in a public place was still sound – and preferable – but if he turned on me and caused a fuss, it might do more harm than good. And, if it made the papers, David wouldn't be too pleased about this kind of attention.

The headline *'Ruckus in Coffee Shop: Do We Really Want to Embrace This Brit?'* streamed through my mind. No, I couldn't risk it. Better that I said what I had to say in the privacy of his apartment. And if he turned on me there? Well, I had my phone and I'd call Blake in a heartbeat if I had to.

*Or the police.*

I arrived at his apartment building with a churning belly and a boatload of determination. Where my dream man was concerned, I was no longer some withering violet, and resolving this issue with Ginger was my top priority. I stepped inside and located a pad on the wall that had names beside each bell. He lived at number fifty-five A, so I jabbed that one and waited for a response. His voice crackled out of the speaker, making me jump even though I'd been expecting it, and I realised I was more nervous than I'd thought.

"It's me, Charlotte," I said. I felt as though I was being watched so glanced around the foyer, but no cameras were in evidence.

*Paranoid much?*

"Oh. Come on up."

A buzzer went off then a clicking sound, and I headed for a glass door off to my left. I found myself in a short hallway with stairs on my right. A metal elevator door stood at the end, and I debated whether to take it. Going up five floors would make me breathless, but I opted to ignore the lift. I needed more time to compose myself.

When I reached the third floor, I regretted my decision. I needed to visit the gym or something. I might well be slim, but fit I was not. I shrugged, ploughing upwards, and by the time I got to Ginger's floor I was panting like I'd run a marathon. I leant against the wall beside his door to steady my breath. Unfortunately for me, he opened it, catching me off guard in what I could only imagine was a bright-red-tomato-caught-in-the-headlights look. My cheeks were hot, and the back of my neck was clammy, my hands too. This detective business was harder than it appeared on TV.

"Are you all right?" he asked.

I lifted my sunglasses and balanced them on top of my head.

He narrowed his eyes in what I prayed was concern and not hope that I was going to pop off this mortal coil within the next minute or so. I knew he wasn't enamoured with me—I'd discovered that when I'd eavesdropped on him and Blake in the past, yet I'd stuck up for him in a conversation with Roo-Roo and wondered why I'd bothered. I had a feeling Ginger thought I was like another woman Blake had had in his life, some famous lady who had scammed Blake out of two million dollars. I wasn't anything like her, and I understood Ginger's concern, but he'd just have to learn that not everyone was out to fleece Blake of his money.

That was rich, if what I suspected of him was true.

"Yes, thanks. I'm fine. Just out of breath, that's all." I gave him a fake smile, big and wide and 'Nothing to see here, you can pretend I don't look like I've been dragged through a hedge backwards'. My smile became genuine then as I recalled when I had been dragged about in a bush after I'd been eavesdropping—again—*do I sense a pattern here?*—on Blake and a woman outside Gianni's restaurant.

"Oh, right." He stared at me as though he thought I was demented. "So long as you're okay, come in."

*Can't I still go in if I'm not okay?*

"I think I'm better off chatting with you here rather than going to the coffee shop," I said. "Feeling a bit faint."

"Whatever." He waved his hand to dismiss me.

I wanted to call him out on being so rude but refrained. Instead I stepped inside and took note of the layout in case I had to scarper once I'd revealed my real reason for being here. That was what cops did, wasn't it, scoped the joint out? His apartment was straightforward, just a stubby hallway with a door either side then a lounge at the end and three more doors on its back wall.

He walked across the cream-painted lounge without saying a word, which felt odd. Then he went through the middle doorway at the back to the kitchen. I followed him. He poured two coffees from a percolator jug like it was the hardest thing he'd ever done, again without speaking, and my detective senses told me he didn't want me here. Well, that was tough, wasn't it? I *was* here and I would say what I'd come to say whether he liked it or not.

He spun to face me with the cups in his hands, and I internally winced as some of the liquid sloshed onto the floor. If I let my imagination do its usual thing, I'd take a guess that he might well throw that hot brew at me if he got angry enough.

*Stop that. You're being silly.*

I took one of the cups. "Thanks. Sorry to be such a pest. You know, by not wanting to go out for our bonding session."

He snorted. "Bonding session? Hardly. I'd have thought you'd have gathered from our recent conversation that you're the last person I'd want to bond with."

He strode off into the lounge, leaving me thinking that he must be either very abrupt in general or incredibly rude. I shrugged it off. Some folks weren't people persons, and if he was one of those then I'd respect that. I didn't have to meet with him alone in future. I'd get this meeting over and done with then hotfoot it back to Blake's.

I went and joined him. He stood beside a white leather sofa, coffee still clutched in his hand. Before I further convinced myself that the cup was a weapon, I sat on one of the recliner chairs, knowing full well he wasn't about to offer me a seat. If he could be rude, so could I.

"What do you want?" he asked, as blunt as Blake but without the finesse.

All right, if he wanted to play it that way, I'd play.

"You know you said you thought I was clever? Well, I think you're right. And I also think you're up to something with Blake's money." I was pleased with myself for sounding so assured, yet was pooping my pants inside.

"Do you now?" he drawled, thankfully placing his cup on a side table then sitting on the sofa. "And how did you come to that conclusion?" He crossed one leg over the other and studied me—hard.

His scrutiny made me feel uncomfortable, but I'd been stared at by a million eyes at once before—some nice, others not so—and I drew on my professional experience in order to deal with it. Basically, I pretended it didn't bother me.

"You were in Blake's office yesterday—and let me tell you, I don't like the fact that you just went in there without knocking on the front door." I felt a babble coming on but didn't care. *Let him have the lot!* "And you lied to him. You said you were at the business office and you weren't. *And* you came into the bedroom and stared at me while I was in bed." I held back a shudder. *Creepy bugger.* "I wasn't asleep, I'd been spying on you the whole time. You moved money that wasn't yours, didn't you?"

I had no idea where that had come from. My subconscious was a funny sod and sometimes didn't let me in on what it was dreaming up. Well, now it had let me know, and my instinct was to think I'd hit the nail on the head, especially because his scrunched-up face turned the same shade as his hair.

"So I was right," I said, denying myself a victory air-punch. "You bastard!" I stood, anger filling me on Blake's behalf, and clenched my fist, alarmed that I wanted to bop him so hard on his nose it would make him cry. Or douse him in my coffee. I kept hold of the cup in case *I* needed it as a weapon. Relieved I'd got my suspicions off my chest, I waited for his excuses.

"So, what are you going to do about it? Run to Blake?" He sneered, the skin on the bridge of his nose turning into a concertina. "He won't entertain your bullshit, you know. Why would he? I'm his *brother,* and you're just some trumped-up famous broad he's infatuated with." He pressed the end of one finger to the side of his mouth.

"Hmm, let's see. Who would you believe? Someone you've known all your life, or someone you've only known around a year or so?" He barked out a spiteful stream of laughter. "Think about that for a second. And while you do, I'm going to use the bathroom."

He walked off casually, as though I'd accused him of nothing more than pinching an apple off a neighbour's tree. And the fact that he'd basically *admitted* it... Bloody hell, I hadn't expected that at all. He had some nerve, didn't he? I stared at his back as he disappeared through one of the doors beside the kitchen, wanting to chase after him and demand more of an answer. More details. Once he'd closed the door, I began worrying. What if he came out of there with a razor? Or...or even the shower hose? He could strangle me with it!

I suddenly wished I hadn't said anything about this situation to him at all.

I paced. I fretted. I tried to work out what to do next. Should I leave, find Blake and tell him what Ginger had said? Or should I stay, fight this out with him, and demand that he return all the money he'd stolen?

The bathroom door opening took my decision away. He walked towards me with a smarmy smile on his face, clearly thinking I'd cower and scuttle off with my tail between my legs.

*Uh, no.*

"Okay, I've thought about it," I said. "And yes, I'm going to tell Blake. He doesn't deserve his brother scamming him. But then you're not really related at all, are you? How much have you taken? Hundreds? Thousands?" I planted one hand on my hip, doing my best to give off an Incredible Hulk vibe.

*Don't push me. You won't like it when I'm angry.*

He laughed. Loud and cruel and mocking. Again I wanted to punch him for being so…so good at being bad. He was a real super villain, while I was just playing at being a super heroine.

"Hundreds? Thousands?" He laughed again.

*May God forgive me if my knee accidentally finds its forceful way to his nether regions.*

"Try millions, lady."

I gasped, couldn't stop it from coming out. Millions? "What?" I was dumbfounded. Words eluded me as my brain tried to digest what he'd said. How had Blake not noticed such a vast amount of money going missing? How long had Ginger been filtering money into his personal account? How had he done it without anything being spotted?

"You heard me, Charlotte. Millions." He sat on the sofa, blasé, drinking his coffee as if what he'd said was nothing.

Hulk pose forgotten, I scrabbled for something scary to say. "I… What… How could you *do* that?"

"How? Oh, that's easy. Overcharging clients. Doctoring the invoices. Paying myself the difference. Do it for long enough and the money soon mounts up. And what better position to be in—no one would suspect a brother, right?"

I stared at him, mouth open, aware a zillion flies could cram inside there if I left it like that any longer. Not that a zillion flies were in the room but—

*Concentrate! Don't let your mind wander.*

"Like no one would suspect a brother of causing a fall on a construction site?" I asked.

He sniffed then gulped his coffee down. "Oh, that. It was nothing."

"Nothing? Trying to cripple or kill your brother is *nothing*?" I was so incensed I wanted to scream.

"Oh, be quiet. As for the money, I'd say 'Come on, work it out', but I guess you might be an airhead after all who needs it *spelling* out. So if you want a lesson in how I do it, I'll gladly give you one."

Why the hell was he confessing this to me? Why wasn't he denying it? Was he so sure of himself and Blake's trust in him that he was absolutely certain I wouldn't be believed?

I was in deeper than I wanted to be, in a position I didn't want to be in. But how could I ignore this and allow that man to continue robbing Blake, to continue being a danger?

"You want in on this, is that it? You want some cash to stop you talking? Fine." He stood, reaching me in two fast strides.

I wanted to whimper but cut it off. I couldn't let him know he was *really* unsettling me now. He was inside my imaginary hula hoop of personal space and he needed to step back.

"Like that other bitch, huh?" He lifted his chin. "Yeah, as I thought, you're just the same as her."

I didn't have to be DI Taylor to work out who he meant. He was referring to that star who had conned the two million. Wait a minute. Had Ginger been in on that too?

"Oh…" I said.

"The penny's dropped, right?" He sniffed again. "You coming into Blake's life really fucked that little scheme up. You cost me another half a mil."

"What do you mean?" Why hadn't I thought to record this conversation on my phone? I wished I'd gone to cop school. I reckoned that would be one of the first things they'd have taught me.

"Don't you remember? That's strange, because I'm sure you were listening to one of my conversations with Blake once. You know, when I told him to pay her more money. We split whatever he gave her fifty-fifty. But you helped him grow a pair of balls and he wouldn't budge on that suggestion. You have a lot to answer for."

"Look, I'm leaving." I had to get away from him. His stinky coffee breath was making me feel queasy, not to mention his blazing eyes and scary aura.

"Just remember," he said, and inched a little closer, "that Blake won't believe you. I'll make sure of that."

"How?" I whispered, dreading his answer.

"By making up so much shit about you that he won't want to be with you anymore. And he won't, you can bet on it. Kicked to the kerb, that's what you'll be. He'll trust me when I tell him what you've been up to."

"But I haven't been up to anything!" I backed away, lifting my cup a bit.

"No, you haven't. I've already had you checked out. But I can make it look like you have. Photoshop is great for image manipulation, after all. And if Blake can fall from scaffolding, just think what a clumsy woman like you could fall from."

"Oh, oh, you…you…"

I dashed the coffee in his face, threw the cup at him, then raced across the room. I turned back to look over my shoulder. Instead of being hunched over and bleating in pain, he was exactly where I'd left him, except he was wet and a red mark was blooming on his cheek.

I dashed down the hallway to the front door. As I swung it open, he called, "If you say anything, you're going to regret what you just did, remember that. Death is forever, lady."

"I won't say anything, I swear!"

And that was all he'd get from me on the subject. I was out of there.

# 18

On the street, I gasped for air and plastered my back to the apartment block wall. I couldn't believe I'd thrown coffee and a cup at him, but it was better than breaking my knuckles by giving him a punch. All the information I'd learned swelled in my head, threatening to fill it so much that it would be all I could think of forevermore. I couldn't let that happen—I had research to do this afternoon on the chat show host, Chiquita. David was meeting me at the studio, and he'd expect me to have watched a few episodes on YouTube so I became familiar with Chiquita's style and whether she was the type to ask leading or damning questions.

But how could I concentrate on that now? How could I even go on a show while my nerves were wrecked? Also, I had another big secret I was planning to keep from Blake. After the last one, we'd promised never to do that again. Yet I was going to, willingly. If I didn't… I didn't doubt Ginger's threats. He'd dream up such a horrible story about me that Blake would run as far away as possible.

Or Ginger would kill me.

Maybe I could alert another member of Blake's staff and they could do a bit of snooping then let Blake know their findings? There had to be some way I could stop his hard-earned money landing in Ginger's bank.

Feeling better for doing something productive about it rather than meekly keeping quiet, I began the walk back to Blake's penthouse. Hopefully he wouldn't be there and I could pootle around by myself, thinking, researching, and trying to get myself calm enough to appear on Chiquita's show tonight.

By the time I let myself inside, I was shaking. I'd had visions of Ginger following me and imagined him whispering behind me that he was going to get me and make me pay. I checked I was alone, locked and chained the door, then made my way to the kitchen, where I poured a large glass of wine and tossed it down. I never usually did that, especially when I had to work, but I had to have something to settle my nerves.

It was either that or crumble.

And I wasn't going to do that.

"So when it's your turn to sit on the sofa, the green light up there will go on and you need to head for the stage entryway. And that's it!"

I stared at the male stagehand, realising I'd only caught the last part of what he'd said. I was aware he'd been speaking for quite a while, but my mind was still full of Ginger. Blake had opted to go back to his place after he'd dropped me off here. He had an appointment with David, who had sent me an email just before I'd left for the studio saying he had a new job in mind for me but that he needed to run it by Blake first. David assured me it was exciting and that I'd love it, so I wrote back asking what it was and what Blake had to do with it, but he hadn't replied by the time I had to leave. Blake said once David left he'd cook us a late dinner so it would be ready for when I was finished, and I was glad. It meant we hadn't had to engage in small talk in the green room, and with me busy getting ready when he'd arrived home, he'd said my lack of input to any conversation he'd tried to have with me was nerves on my part.

I hadn't put him straight on that.

"Oh, okay," I said, inwardly shaking myself out of earlier events and into the now.

I had a job to do, and after David's phone call earlier, telling me I had a surprise in store on the show tonight, I really needed to concentrate. David said he'd meet me at the aftershow party so he could mingle and possibly get me even more work. I had jobs coming out of my ears already, but it was important to keep my name and face in the spotlight.

I slipped off my Charlotte mantle and swamped myself in Lola. Immediately, a sense of being in control filled me, and I straightened out my slumped shoulders, feeling a little lighter of heart. I'd deal with the Ginger Saga another day.

As for the surprise, I could only imagine. My research on Chiquita had thrown up a few episodes that proved she was outrageous, flamboyant, and thought nothing of pushing the boundaries, and her guests. I'd need all my mettle to get through the next twenty minutes.

Another man came in, and he ushered me to the stage entrance, even though the green light hadn't come on. Or had it, and I'd been too preoccupied to notice?

I took a deep breath and smiled at him. He held my elbow in a light grip then gently pushed me forward.

*Okay, you can do this, Lola. You're a professional and it's nothing you can't handle.*

"And now," came a disembodied male voice that would have sounded better as a horror-movie announcer than one for a night-time show, "the Brit singing sensation, Lola!"

The audience clapped and cheered, whooping like teenagers let out after they'd been grounded. I walked onto the set, recognising the long guest sofa from the YouTube videos, and Chiquita's large, ornate mahogany desk. She sat behind it, a tanned, forty-something queen, all regal bearing, an assured woman who had oodles of self-belief. A Carmen Miranda ensemble sat on her head—a whole bowl of plastic fruit if I was any judge—and I wondered if the weight of it gave her neck ache. The sequins on her bright pink dress sparkled under the lights, and honestly, she looked so beautiful that I felt drab in comparison wearing my boring black dress and sling-back heels.

I smiled and waved at the audience, and she rose from her throne to give me a hug and two air kisses. She smelled gorgeous, and I was glad she liked floral perfume. I'd brought a bottle of Daydreamer with me to offer her as a gift.

"Welcome, darling," she said, waving the same way as our dear Queen Elizabeth II. "So lovely to have you here."

"Lovely to be here. Thank you for having me."

I noticed the two other guests I'd previously seen in the green room. I hadn't introduced myself to them, what with being so distracted. They shifted along the sofa to allow me some room and I sat closest to Chiquita. I had no idea who they were or what they did so smiled at them too. One was a distinguished-looking old man, and the other a young woman about the same age as me, with penny-sized piercings in her cheeks that showed the inside of her mouth.

*Ow?*

I turned away to face Chiquita, and she beamed at me, her perfect teeth putting Johnny Bravo's to shame. Her barrage of questions were what I'd expected, so it put me at ease and I realised I hadn't needed to research her after all.

"So," she said, once I'd told her about my album, the Daydreamer fragrance and, of course, my tale about singing on Tube platforms and how I'd become famous, "since you've been such a charming guest, I think I want *you* to play our celebrity game tonight." She gave the other two stars on the sofa a disparaging look, as though they hadn't been as interesting as she would have liked.

From what I'd gleaned earlier, The Chiquita Show always had a game for the celebs to play. The one I'd seen on YouTube was charades with blindfolds. How hard could that be? I nodded, eager to please her and the viewers, and she clapped manically, bouncing in her seat.

"Oh, you're *such* a doll!" she said. "I knew I could count on you."

She handed me a blindfold, and I relaxed further, content that I could act out a song or movie title without being able to see. I caught sight of two runners bringing in a table covered with a cloth—a cloth that was hiding things beneath it.

*This doesn't look like charades. Oh my God, what have I let myself in for?*

Chiquita came out from behind her desk, her long dress swishing around her ankles. Her glorious headgear swayed as she walked, and I believed it was in danger of wobbling off.

"Come," she said. "Come and sit over here."

I obeyed—how could I not?—and let her push me into a seat behind the table. She took the blindfold from me then placed it over my eyes amid *oohs* and *ahhs* from the audience.

"A new game, my beautiful people, played for the very first time by the amazing Lola!"

*Seriously, what the hell is this? Why didn't I research better or listen to that man in the green room better? I could have signed myself up for all sorts here!*

Chiquita rested her hands on my shoulders, giving me a bit of a fright.

"We thought a new game was in order," Chiquita said. "And I just know you're dying to hear what it's called, right? *Right*?"

"Right!" The audience yelled.

"I thought so. Now, y'all are going to love me for thinking this one up." She took a hand off one of my shoulders, and a snapping sound cracked beside my ear. "You lovely boys, when I give the signal, I want you to remove that cloth." She paused, waiting for the audience to finish *oohing*. "Now, you guys, you're going to see what's under this cloth any second now, but remember, keep it quiet. Lola here mustn't know what we're up to!"

My stomach muscles tightened and I breathed deeply. If I got up now and refused to play, it would make me seem childish. I had to be a good sport about this, much as I wished the night was over already.

The cloth must have been swished away, because the audience went wild. I wondered if someone was standing in front of them with a card that said they had to make vomiting noises and the loudest groans possible.

*What the…?*

*It's only five minutes of your life. Come on, you can get through this.*

"So, you want to know what this game is called, y'all?" Chiquita asked.

"Yeah!" came the unanimous audience response.

"You ready for this?" Chiquita paused. "Iiiiiiiiittt's Crunch Time!"

*Oh my bloody days…*

That didn't sound promising at all.

"I recently went abroad to Asia," Chiquita said. "And they eat the darnedest things. So I *cooked* this little game up, among other things." She waited for the audience to stop laughing. "And now here we are! Lola, I want you to try a few *delicacies*." The audience roared again. "Foods you might not ordinarily choose to eat. Are you up for that?"

That didn't sound so bad. I could handle a few Brussel sprouts or a bit of sloppy cabbage. Even a mouldy slice of bread at a push. "Okay…"

"Good girl, I *knew* you were the right choice." Chiquita squeezed my shoulder then took her hand away.

I felt strangely alone yet very watched. The audience had gone silent. Then I heard something being scraped, maybe a plate, and the sound of cutlery on china. I got myself ready to be fed, which was odd all by itself, and waited for the first bite.

"Here comes the first delicacy," Chiquita said. "Open up!"

I did as she'd asked, and it tasted and felt like pâté. Noises from the audience assured me I was eating something horrific, though. Either that or the sound man was holding up a card again.

"So, what do you think that is?" Chiquita demanded.

"Pâté?"

The audience bellowed out laughter.

"All right..." Chiquita giggled. "On to the next."

The second mouthful had the texture of an elastic band and tasted like chicken, but it took me ages to chew and after a while, when my jaw started aching, I contemplated asking if I could spit it out.

"You've got to swallow it!" Chiquita said.

I managed to do just that without choking. "Chicken, turkey, something like that?"

"Ha ha! *And* the next!"

This one was crunchy and tasted pretty good, so I had no trouble eating it. The audience made those sicky noises again, but none of the delicacies tasted as bad as they seemed to think they should. Maybe I was eating *really* gross stuff and if I'd known what they were I wouldn't have touched them let alone allowed them in my mouth.

"Pork scratching?" I said.

"Say what now?" Chiquita asked. She clamped her hand back on my shoulder.

"Pork rinds," I amended, remembering the differences between the UK and US.

"Oh, *Lord* above! Pork rinds! Aha! Ha!"

Okay, so it clearly wasn't pork. "Can I take my blindfold off now?"

"You surely can, sugar!"

I whipped it off, placing it on the table that held three plates covered with silver domes. Three cards stood in front of the domes, and I guessed that was how the audience knew what I'd been eating—the name of the delicacy was probably written on them. Chiquita quickly picked them up and held them to her ample bosom then guided me out of my seat to walk around to the front of the table.

"Let's look at the first one, honey."

She lifted the dome and, as I'd thought, pâté in a little ceramic bowl.

"You want to know what you ate?" she asked.

"Yes, please," although I really didn't. I had a feeling I was better off not knowing.

She brandished one of the cards, shoving it so close to my face I couldn't read it at first. I focused and, to my horror, read *PIG BRAINS!*

*Oh…oh oh oh!*

I swallowed, feeling bile rising. Then she took the second dome off with an almost menacing flourish, obviously enjoying herself. I stared down at what looked like a piece of gristle. Another card was floated before my eyes.

*KANGAROO PENIS!*

*Oh wow. Okay. Oh wow again.*

I smiled, letting out the appropriate groan, my cheeks growing hot, and prepared myself for the final reveal. It appeared to be crispy black slices of something, small, about the size of a fifty pence piece. I tilted my head, trying to work it out, then Chiquita thrust the last card at me.

*BAKED TARANTULA!*

That was it. I willed away my need to be sick, or to run, as though the tarantula was alive and ready to chase me. I did not do spiders, alive or dead, and eating a part of one wasn't something I'd ever intended to do. And I'd thought it was as yummy as a pork scratching too!

"Oh, you brave, brave girl!" Chiquita crooned, massaging circles on my back as though it would stop me being ill.

Then she abandoned me to walk to the edge of the set, standing in front of the audience with her arms out at her sides.

"And that," she declared, "is Crunch Time! Thank you to my wonderful guests – the ever lovely Marcos De Fringla, Sherry Spangles, and the most utterly charming and greatest sport ever, y'all, Lola, who is now going to sing her little old heart out for us!"

# 19

After I'd belted out my latest single, I watched the credits rolling on the screen to Chiquita's right. The applause from the audience made me feel a little better. I'd given them entertainment, and that was what I'd focus on, not the fact that I probably still had animal penis on my tongue.

Stage hands came by to escort us off set and into the green room, and I lunged for the water cooler, pouring out a large cup and drinking it down then swishing it around to get rid of anything left in my mouth. I dumped the cup in the bin, looking around to see if David had arrived yet. He hadn't, so I stood there feeling a Billy No Mates.

Then Sherry Spangles came up beside me and nudged me in the ribs. "You've earned major points with Chiquita. That's a huge thing over here. And the audience loved you. I'd say you got it made, darlin'."

"Thank you," I said, glad to be able to forget the delicacies for a moment.

"It takes some balls to do what you did," she went on. "I wouldn't have done it. Bit of a rebel. I like to fight against the system." She laughed and pointed at her piercings. "But I see now why she asked you. Old De Fringla would most likely have needed the Heimlich manoeuvre if he'd eaten that kanga dick—it looked like it was real hard to chew, babe—and if I'd eaten the pig brains it would have squirted out the sides of my face."

I nodded and giggled, dying to ask why she'd had her face pierced like that but thinking it might be seen as rude. If I'd been concentrating before my spot on the show, I could have watched her interview on the green room TV and would probably know all about her. Before she could explain anything about herself—if she even planned to—we were interrupted by David calling out my name.

Relieved he'd turned up, I turned to Sherry. "Sorry, I need to speak with my manager. It was lovely to meet you."

"Great to meet you too. I'll be sure to buy your records."

"Thank you!"

I moved towards David, shuddering as I remembered what was swirling round in my belly, and he grinned.

"You bloody knew, didn't you?" I stood in front of him and grinned back. "David! The things I do!"

"You were superb. I haven't laughed so much in ages. I got to watch it out in the lobby." His facial expression turned serious. "Listen, much as I like fun and games, I have some business to discuss with you before you see Blake. I offered to drop you at his place, by the way."

I glanced around the green room, surprised at how it had filled up with people—set hands and camera men, I assumed. Chiquita held court on one corner, her headdress removed, long wavy hair cascading down her back. It was glorious and shiny, each tress catching the light.

"Okay, no one's around us, so will here do?"

"No, I'd prefer to chat in the car if you don't mind. I know I said I wanted to mingle here for a while, but the project I mentioned in my email is exciting and I want to know how you feel about it. I can drop you at Blake's then come back here to do some networking."

We left the venue after I'd given my usual polite excuses used on occasions like this, and I'd handed Chiquita a large bottle of Daydreamer. David lost no time once we were in his hire car to lay it all out.

"So I went to see Blake tonight," he said.

I frowned. "And?"

"I put it to him that I want you to be the face promoting his latest venture." David stopped at a red light. The hue of it gave him an ominous glow.

"What?" I widened my eyes and stared ahead.

I thought about how that famous woman who had tricked Blake out of that two million with Ginger was also meant to have been the face of one of his new ventures. David asking him if I could do the same kind of job wasn't something I thought he'd have done. Plus, if this got out to Ginger, I had a feeling he might tell Blake I was just like her and only wanted Blake so I could get a similar job on one of his new buildings. That most certainly wasn't true, but now that David had suggested it, I wouldn't blame Blake if he thought otherwise.

"You're annoyed with me," David stated as he pulled across the intersection.

I whipped my head around to face him. "Of course I'm annoyed. This is the one job I would *not* want to do, David. I'm sure I told you before that Blake had his trust well and truly broken by another woman over a job just like this one, so the last thing I'd want to do is be the face of this new venture because it makes it look like that's what I've been after all along." I fumed, words queuing up in my mouth, itching to burst out. "You should have told me right from the start what you wanted to talk to him about and I could have told you not to bother. But well done you, he's going to think this was all planned now. I'm not doing that bloody job, even if he's told you he'd like me to. It's the principle of the thing. I don't need the strain it might put on our relationship. But oh, that's already been done, because you can bet he's upset right now, thinking I've played him. Thanks. Thanks very much."

Wow, I'd never spoken to David like that before, but the idea that what he'd done might put a spanner in the works really set my nerves on edge. I wanted to get out of the car and run, reach Blake as quickly as I could so I could make everything all right again.

"I didn't think you'd mind," David said. "Kind of like you'd be working together on something. I'm really sorry if I stepped out of line. I had no idea you'd feel this strongly. He's building a massive music arena, Lola. He wasn't against the idea of you being the face of it."

"I don't give a toss! It's not the actual job that's the problem. It's the idea this was planned from the start. Don't talk to me anymore tonight, David. Just don't."

We continued the drive in silence, and by the time I leapt out of the car outside Blake's apartment block, I felt like I was being strangled. I couldn't breathe with the intensity of my fury, and I slammed the car door, not looking back as I ran inside the building. The elevator seemed to take forever, further increasing my anger and impatience, and once I reached the penthouse and stormed inside, I should have had Hulky green skin and clothes hanging off me in ripped shreds.

I stopped short, staring down at Blake, who sat on the sofa in the sunken area. The door closed behind me, and I stepped forward, suddenly worried by the reception I was going to get.

He never said a word and didn't acknowledge I was there in any way.

"I didn't know," I said. "I swear to you, I didn't know that he'd ask you…*that*."

"I seriously hope you're telling me the truth," he said, too quietly, too controlled.

I rushed down the steps to sit beside him, taking his hand in both of mine and wishing he'd turn to look at me so he could see the sincerity I hoped was plastered all over my face.

"I promise you I didn't know. I don't want that job and I told David as much. I didn't even know you were building an arena until David just told me. So unless you think David told me before tonight… All I got was an email from him saying he had a job for me and that he wanted to run it by you first. Please believe me. Please. Look, I'll ring David right now on speakerphone and chew him out. I've already done that in the car but I'll do it again. Anything to prove to you I didn't know what job he had planned."

"That's not necessary," he said. "I can tell you're not lying."

"Oh, thank God… I'm so annoyed I can't think straight."

"Come here." Blake held one arm out.

I all but lunged at him, pressing myself so close, hugging him hard and thanking my lucky stars he knew I wasn't capable of being so conniving. But my thoughts quickly went back to bad ones. I thought of whether Ginger had pondered aloud to Blake about me possibly being the face of the music arena, and it reopened that ugly can of worms involving Tangerine Man, which now writhed in my head, poisoning my brain with a fresh reminder of what he'd done to Blake. I clamped my mouth shut to make sure I didn't blab it all out, and told myself that I'd rat that little weasel out somehow, just not now.

He cupped my cheek, and the warmth of his palm was so welcome, so what I needed. He stared at me, as though convincing himself one final time that I was telling the truth. It must have been difficult for him. I'd lied by omission in the past, but then so had he. He dipped his head, brushing his lips against mine. I was tempted to shut my eyes, to revel in this moment, pinning it to a notice board in my head where I could think about it in the years to come and smile, but at the same time I wanted to keep them open to see if he closed his.

He did, and so I followed his lead, sinking into a deeper kiss that curled my toes and tightened my tummy. This—this was what mattered, not other people poking their noses in and spoiling what we had. I didn't think anyone believed the road to true love was smooth, but we were hitting too many potholes along the way, ones I didn't think we deserved. All we wanted was to be together, happy and secure. Maybe this trust thing—complete trust—would take time. Maybe we just had to roll with the punches and get through the best way we could.

He slid his hand from my cheek, down to my throat, resting his thumb on the ticking beat of my pulse. I spread one hand out on his chest and convinced myself our hearts were thudding as one.

Moving his hand lower, he crested my collarbone and stayed his palm on my chest. I pushed myself closer and gripped his top in my fist, kissing him harder. His arm behind me tightened our embrace and, locked together like that, no one else existed in my world but us.

He broke the spell, shifting away from me then standing, holding both hands out. I took them in mine and he pulled me up, kissing me the second our bodies came into contact again. He slipped his hands around my waist, moving them lower, then drew me even closer. I gasped, gazing into his eyes, wanting to say something yet nothing at all. I couldn't let a stream of babble out and spoil this special moment. It felt like silence was needed, a connection where our bodies did all the talking, and our souls entwined, fusing us, bonding us forever.

Blake lifted a hand and stroked the back of one finger down my cheek. He parted his lips, as if about to say something. I shook my head, an almost imperceptible gesture, and he remained quiet, just looking at me, his feelings displayed in those beautiful eyes of his.

He loved me. Adored me. And I'd never felt it as keenly as I did now. I'd thought before that moments like this couldn't get any better, that the love I felt for him was as big and wide and tall and all-encompassing as it was going to get, but each new moment brought new experiences, drowning out the previous with its enormity.

Would I feel more in the future? Something bigger than even this? I was already bursting at the seams with it, so much so that I didn't know what to do with it all.

*I love you so much. I can't…*

Tears stung my eyes. I blinked, and Blake traced his finger across my cheek again, to my lips. He pressed the pad of it to my mouth, holding back the words I'd thought, as though he'd already heard them and I didn't need to repeat them out loud.

"I know," he whispered. "I know."

I smoothed my hands over his chest, spanning my fingertips over his collarbone. He ghosted his finger from my mouth to the hollow at my throat, circling the dip softly, until goosebumps raced over my skin. I breathed heavily, suspended in the kind of moment I'd dreamed of most of my adult life. This had to be incredibly special. Did everyone feel this way when they were in love—truly in love?

He swept me up in his arms then, carrying me up the sunken steps, and I clutched him around the neck. He walked to the bedroom, all the while looking down at me as I looked up at him. I held on tight as he lowered me to the mattress, pulling him down so his body covered mine. Every part of me wanted him—wanted that union where love and desire combined to make a heady concoction that robbed me of the ability to breathe.

The weight of him shifted as he braced his hands on the mattress either side of me and lifted his torso. I still hung on to his neck, unwilling to let him go.

"I'm not going anywhere," he said.

Then he lowered his head, kissing me tenderly, and took me to that beautiful place where passion ignited, burning brightly then fizzling out to leave me sated, happy and contented.

**Diary**

**Am I Alive?**

I have nothing. No more words, comparisons or explanations for the way I feel right now. Each and every care in my little world has disappeared. I have just the hollow sound of silence running through my often congested brain. Pure and sincere happiness. I didn't know this state of mind existed. My entire presence is like jelly.

How did I get this lucky? I feel as though I've won! If it all ended right here, right now, it wouldn't matter because I've experienced the highest form of happiness possible.

I'm floating. I've become a weightless spirit floating through life, beaming an incredible light. Am I even here? Have I literally died and gone to Heaven?

Either way, alive or dead, I'm in love and it feels good!

# 20

A lovely new day. A clean page and a chance to put the bad things behind me for a while. In a couple of hours I had an interview on one of the local radio stations, but for now I'd be walking with Blake to his office block. The final hours of last night had been so beautiful that I didn't want anything to taint my dreamy mood, so I clutched his hand and cast my mind back to when Blake had been my guide when I'd first come to New York. We'd hailed a taxi to sightsee, and it had been a revelation as to how big this place actually was. It would take me a long time to know exactly where to go without Blake giving me directions, but I was confident I'd manage to get to where the radio station was by myself. Blake had insisted on taking me, but like I'd said to him, he couldn't hold my hand all the time. David had also checked in via phone earlier, offering to pick me up, but I'd been curt with him and said I didn't need him to hold my hand at every job either.

I was finally growing some balls. As for me being recognised by the public, my sunglasses and big floppy hat had seemed to work wonders so far. I'd slip them on while I walked to the station.

At the main doors of Blake's office building, he took me in his arms and hugged me close.

"You'll be okay, won't you?" he asked. "I can defer my meeting until after the radio show if you need me to."

"No, I'll be fine." I appreciated his protective streak more than he knew—true knight in shining armour right there.

"Okay, so long as you're sure." He slid one finger beneath my chin and tipped my head back. "I could kiss you right here on the street."

"So kiss me."

I smiled as his lips met mine, loving the way it felt as though we were alone, no one else occupying the street on their way to work. At times like this, everything was all right with my world and I wished it could always be that way. But with people in my life like Ginger, that would never be the case.

"Blake, really!"

*Speak of the devil and he shall appear…*

I sprang away from Blake, fear setting up a fierce boil inside me. Ginger stood there staring at me, a dark bruise covering his cheekbone and temple, nasty little glints in his eyes that left nothing to the imagination. If Blake cared to look close enough, he'd see his so-called brother hated my guts. The feeling was more than mutual, but I had to play my cards close to my chest. I'd act as if nothing had been said between us, giving Blake no reason to believe Ginger if he decided he'd let my dream man know about our horrid conversation.

"What, never kissed the love of your life in the street before?" Blake asked. "Oh, I forgot, you've never had a love of your life."

Ginger's face turned red, and I was glad. Blake had hit a nerve and in doing so had given me ammunition. I filed it to save for later.

"Har har, very funny," Ginger said in his usual drawl. "I need to have a chat with you as soon as you can pry yourself away from *her*."

*Ooh!* He'd let his real feelings show in front of Blake. If he wanted to alienate Blake, he was going the right way about it. Blake gave him a frigid stare and pulled me to his side. I smirked at Ginger, unable to stop myself, and he glared at me for a moment before giving Blake his attention.

"Yes, you might well stare at me like that, brother." Ginger puffed out his chest. "But you don't know what I discussed with her during our little coffee time chat. Unless she's told you her version, which, of course, will be a load of bullshit."

*What's Ginger playing at?*

Blake stiffened. I hadn't said anything to him about my conversation with Connor—even to say it went fine. There hadn't been the time and Blake hadn't asked. I'd been grateful for that because it meant I hadn't had to lie.

"Just who the hell do you think you are?" Blake said, taking a step towards Ginger and pushing me behind him.

Although touched by his protection, I wasn't going to stay out of the way. I was ready to scratch Ginger's eyes out since he'd obviously planned to play dirty, consequences or not. And if I had to, I'd give a shout out to what he'd been doing with Blake's money for years—in front of Blake so I could watch Ginger deny it. I should do that, right this second. And mention the scaffolding. And our little chat in Gianni's.

Filled with courage and indignation, I opened my mouth.

"Did you know she wants to be the face of your new venture?" Ginger sniffed.

How had he found out about that? If he was asking Blake, it meant Blake hadn't told him. So that only left David.

*Oh no, please don't tell me he's gone behind my back to Ginger as well…*

*Unless Ginger is bluffing.*

"Who told you that?" Blake snapped and took hold of Ginger's jacket lapel.

Ginger shrugged him off, walking backwards to the office block. "Wouldn't you like to know?"

He glanced meaningfully at me, and I couldn't keep my mouth shut any longer.

"Don't you look at me like that." I stalked out from behind Blake. "I haven't spoken to you since our coffee meeting."

"And your point is?" Ginger turned and quickly entered the building.

Blake stared at me, face flushed, his fists clenched. "Tell me he's trying to get a rise out of me. What did he mean by that? What happened at the coffee meeting?"

I had to skirt over the meeting question. "I don't know what he's doing, but I'm telling you now, Blake, if he keeps this shit stirring up, I'm going to have to insist we don't talk about him—ever. I don't like him, he doesn't like me. It's clear he's going to do whatever he can to split us up." I grabbed his hand. "If you want him to succeed with that, believe what he tells you, but if you know me or him at all, you'll know he's just feeding you a line. And he's dangerous. I'll prove it to you if I have to. I will *not* let him come between us."

I must have sounded sincere, possibly even fierce, because Blake hugged me to him, wrapping his arms around my back and squeezing tight. I should have felt safe and warm, embraced like that on a chilly American street, but I didn't. I was cold as stone inside and out, trying not to think of whether this would be the last time Blake held me this way. Ginger was a master at hiding things, at lying, at getting people to believe him. Looking at the odds, I didn't stand a chance against him, but if I went down, I'd go down fighting.

"I'm going to have it out with him," he said. "You have a little time to kill before your interview. Wait for me in my office and I'll come get you when I'm done. I don't want you walking to the station. Not now, not when you're vulnerable."

*Oh, I love him.*

He led the way inside, waving at a receptionist behind a chest-high desk, then strode up a wide flight of stairs to the left. His office sat at the top, and I went inside, taking a seat behind his desk.

"We didn't talk about that job," I said quietly.

He closed the door to and looked at me. "I know."

"So who told him? David?" I frowned. "And why would he do that? David doesn't even know him."

"I don't have a clue but I aim to find out."

*Has Ginger bugged Blake's apartment?*

No, my imagination was going way too far. Wasn't it?

Blake smiled and shrugged. "Listen, Herman, I know Connor. I know what he's like. He's done this kind of thing to me before. He's a spoilt brat, always has been, and anything I have, he wants. Granted, this is a bigger game he's playing here, and I suspect he thinks he's going to win it. But what he doesn't know is the stakes are higher this time. So high he can't even begin to see the top. Do you understand what I'm trying to say?"

I thought I did, so I nodded.

"He doesn't realise just how much I love you. And I probably shouldn't say this because I'll be leaving myself wide open, but even if you did tell him and you lied to me that you didn't…" He paused. "I'll still love you. I'll still want to spend the rest of my life with you."

He walked out before I had a chance to reply, but I knew he'd seen the tears in my eyes. Just to be told he knew what Ginger was like gave me hope. If I had to end up telling Blake about the money laundering and that his accident hadn't really been an accident, he would undoubtedly look into it. Who knew, the seed of doubt might have already been planted on the cash. Blake had seen the windows open on that computer for himself, and I just knew that two different banks being displayed meant something to him.

I swiped at my wet cheeks, blew out a shaky breath, and told myself to buck up. I wasn't about to cry out my relief in this office. No, I was going to go all DI Taylor again and see if I could find out where Blake had gone.

I edged out of the room, spying two doors to my left. Each had a plaque on them, so I sidled along to read the first.

*Secretary.*

I shuffled along some more, careful not to let my heels tap the floor, and found the other door ajar.

*Accounting.*

I held my breath, sure Blake and Ginger were inside. Since meeting Blake, I seemed to have done a lot of spying and eavesdropping. Normally, it wouldn't sit well with me, but I was fighting for my good name here, for my life, *and* to be able to live with my Mr Perfect without trust issues being the elephant in every room we went in together.

I slowly let out some air. I *had* to know first-hand what this ginger weasel was going to feed into Blake's mind, so I moved closer, peering round the doorframe and through the crack.

Blake stood in front of a desk. Ginger sat behind it.

"So are you just going to stand there silent all day?" Ginger asked, swinging back and forth on his chair, ankle propped on his knee.

*Ooh, I could throw coffee on him all over again.*

Blake didn't answer.

"Aren't you even going to ask why I have this black eye?" Ginger pointed to it, as if it made it more obvious the bruise was there.

"I guess you probably pissed someone off. Again. It's not the first bruise you've had on your face." Blake sounded bored. Weary.

"*She* did it," Ginger said. He propelled himself out of his chair then walked around to stand in front of Blake. "Look at it. Look what she did."

Blake drew his lips inwards over his teeth.

"Don't you laugh now," Ginger said. "The love of your life is a nasty little witch."

"Hey." Blake held up one finger. "If you can't keep it civil, I don't want to hear what you have to say. Be careful how you speak about her. I won't warn you again, understand?"

"Oh, yeah, I forgot. You're Superman."

Instantly, I thought of what Blake had told me about his childhood and the Swarovski crystal.

"So what is she now, your Kryptonite?" Ginger huffed out a laugh. "You're a joke, you know that? She's got you right where she wants you, and by the time she's finished with you it'll be too late. You'll have married her, had a kid, and all your money will be gone. Prenuptial is the word of the week here. Listen to me, man. I told you what that last bitch was like and you didn't listen. Are you going to make the same mistake again? Are you going to think with your dick and not your brain?"

"Charlotte's not like that. You don't know her." Blake lowered his finger, jamming his thumb in his waistband.

"And after having coffee thrown in my face by her, I don't *want* to know her."

"Say what?" Blake said on a laugh.

I smiled, wanting to laugh with him.

Ginger pushed his chin up. "She threw *coffee* in my *face*." He shook his head a bit. "*And* the cup."

Blake let out a roar of laughter, walking away from Ginger and towards the door. I got ready to scoot, thinking I could make it back to his office before he saw me.

"This conversation is over." Blake presented his back to the door. "For Charlotte to have done that—and she is in no way a vindictive or aggressive person—you had to have upset her. What did you say to her before she did that, huh? What did you provoke her with?"

Ginger jutted his chest out, resembling an angry orangutan. "She offered to give me half the money for that music arena job if I convinced you she was the right face for it."

I wished I could see Blake's face.

"I said no way," Ginger continued, "and she saw red. Threw the coffee. Then when I told her I was going to let you know what she'd done, she launched the cup at me. I'm telling you, she's fierce when she gets going. If you value your balls, don't annoy her. She'd cut them off while you slept."

"I'd bloody cut *yours* off, you lying little toerag," I muttered.

*Shit…*

"Did you hear that?" Ginger asked.

I scarpered back to Blake's office, zooming across the carpet then flinging myself into his chair. My heart rate went crazy, and I blew air out then dragged it back in, attempting to get myself under control.

Then I stared at the wall, at a painting I guessed Blake had done of the Queensboro Bridge, and studied it nonchalantly while waiting for his return.

# 21

Ginger came bursting in, quickly followed by Blake. I ogled them in shock, as though surprised by their somewhat aggressive entrance. The men stared at one another. Ginger looked defeated, Blake smug. Then Ginger stormed out, slamming the door behind him.

"Is everything all right?" I asked, thinking I'd better play innocent.

"No, everything is *not* all right, but that's for me to sort out. You need to get to that radio station."

I glanced at my watch. "I have another hour or so before I have to be on air if you need to talk about anything?"

"Why, are you worried because I've been talking to Connor?" he snapped.

Er, wow? Why was he angry with me? Did he believe Ginger or something?

"I'm not worried that you've been talking to him at all," I said. "Whatever he's told you about that meeting is a load of rubbish. I've said to you already, not even half an hour ago outside, that he's trying to cause trouble between us. I also told you I'd prove it somehow—and I will, you know."

"So you didn't throw coffee and a cup in his face?" He lifted his eyebrows in his usual way, hands clenched by his sides.

"Yes, I did that. Because he's hateful and threatened me."

Blake's face seemed to cloud over. His eyes narrowed with raw hate and confusion. "Threatened you?"

I leant forwards in the chair and propped my elbows on his desk, holding my face in my hands. I wanted to project a calm, unfazed demeanour, so he'd see I wasn't flustered, therefore, I couldn't possibly be lying. "Yes, he threatened me. To keep my mouth shut about what I know—and I know more than I care to, more than you."

"Tell me what happened."

I'd like to think I'd learned a thing or two in the past. When I'd lied to Blake about being famous at home—okay, I'd just not told him, I didn't outright lie—I'd promised myself I wouldn't lie to him again. Yet I'd fallen into the same pattern here, not lying, but I was keeping something from him again. Both times it was for the same reason—because I was scared of losing him. In this instance, I was allowing Ginger to win until I could prove he'd been stealing. I was allowing his threats of manipulating photos, making things up about me, and outright killing me affect the way I behaved. In short, his scare tactics had worked. But it seemed he was intent on playing hardball anyway. He wasn't going to just continue stealing Blake's money quietly, as though I didn't know anything about it. No, he wanted me out of the picture, and his behaviour in his office and at Gianni's proved that.

So if he was playing dirty, why shouldn't I?

And if Blake believed him? Well, did I want to be with someone who didn't trust me? Much as I adored Blake, much as being without him would all but kill me, did I want to compromise my beliefs like that?

What Blake had said earlier floated into my mind. *'But even if you did tell him and you lied to me that you didn't? I'll still love you. I'll still want to spend the rest of my life with you.'*

I hadn't thought about that properly until now, but what he'd basically said was, even if he believed Ginger and thought I'd lied, that was okay, he'd still want to be with me.

No. That wasn't good. I wanted complete trust, not Blake harbouring doubts throughout our relationship. So, either way, whether I told him about what Ginger had done or not, I might lose Blake anyway.

An inkling of a plan to fix this invaded my head so, with that course of action put to one side for a moment, I decided to come clean.

"Tell you what happened?" I stood, going round to the other side of the desk and perching my backside on it. "All right, but I know already you're going to question it, that although you say you're aware of what Connor's like, you'll still have blinkers on where he's concerned. I understand that, I really do, but if you're prepared to believe him over me—and I understand how you might do that too, what with that other star doing what she did—then I think, after I've told you everything I know, we might need some time apart."

Panic flashed over his face. "What do you mean?"

And I knew right there and then that yes, he'd stay with me whether he believed me or not. That he was a forgiver by nature. I just hoped he'd be able to forgive himself once this conversation was over. He wasn't in that place yet where he totally trusted what I had to say. And that hurt. He was still stuck in the land of family loyalty and brotherly love, despite suspecting Ginger had tried to hurt him on that construction site. And that was okay too. Time apart would make him realise that in the end.

"What I mean is, if, after I tell you about that little chat over coffee, you turn around and say you don't believe what I've said, then time apart is needed. There is no way I can stay around with you supporting that man. You'll need some space to process a few things you refuse to accept at the moment—and if I get lucky, you'll look into what I tell you and discover the truth. After that, when you realise you were wrong, well, I'll be waiting in London and we can take it from there. *If* you come to your senses."

"Oh, so it's ultimatum time, is it?" He had a nasty sneer on his face.

And I didn't like it—it didn't jive with what he'd said about loving me no matter what. Everyone had different sides to them, I knew that, but this one of his wasn't something I wanted to see. It said so much. That he possibly thought I was a manipulator, a woman who wheedled to get what she wanted. Yet he'd told Ginger I wasn't a vindictive person, so what on earth was going on here?

At one time I would have begged and pleaded with Blake for him to believe me, but now? No, I really had grown a set of balls, and if I'd learned anything while being with him, it was that *I* mattered. That I shouldn't allow myself to be led by what other people wanted. I should do what felt right, what I was comfortable with, and never just obey because that's what was expected. Even David was at it, going behind my back and asking Blake about that job.

Well, no more. I intended to stand up for myself. If Blake really was my soulmate, things would work out for the better. No one needed to know that when I went home and closed my front door I would be crying my eyes out behind it again. That I'd be an agonised mess, hoping and praying he'd come knocking on the door like he'd done before.

And if he didn't realise what Ginger was really like? If he didn't come for me?

Then I'd have to learn to deal with it.

"Not ultimatum time, no," I said. "I'm just letting you know that I don't intend to be walked over by some ginger little weasel who is so jealous of you and what you have, he can't help but try to kill you—and steal from you."

"Oh, for crying out loud, we're going down that route again?" He shook his head.

Blimey, he was stubborn. Blinkered. Headstrong. Annoying. Couldn't see the woods for the trees.

*Just like me.*

And, oh, I loved him. All of him. But I also loved myself.

I sighed. "I see you're already refusing to believe, yet you've mentioned your thoughts to me on the 'accident'. So there isn't anything else for it really, is there? I'll lay it out very quickly for you, then I have to get to work. As you know, I'm doing a live radio performance. And thank goodness it's my last job here for a while. London seems to be the safest place for me at the moment."

"Maybe it is." He turned his back on me.

Great. I wouldn't be able to see his face when I told him. Perhaps it was better that way. Then I wouldn't see the hurt.

Ghosts of the past danced between us.

"Right. Connor admitted he's stolen millions from you. For years. He's been fiddling the accounts. And he went halves with that woman—the one who scammed you. They were in it together. Now, even if you don't believe me, there's got to be a niggle of doubt going on inside you. Why would I say something like this if there wasn't proof hidden somewhere that I'm telling the truth? Why would I make up something so outrageous when, after you look into it, it would become obvious that I was a liar? Think about that while I'm gone, will you? That's all I ask."

I pushed myself off the desk then strode to the door. Well now, wasn't that a turn up for the books? I wasn't prepared to walk the line. I wasn't prepared to just do as I was told all in the name of love. What I *was* prepared to do was fight for the kind of love that was crystal clear and without skeletons in closets.

"So you're leaving straight after the radio gig?" he asked, keeping his back to me. "Just like that?"

"I'd have been going back after that anyway. You know I have work lined up back home. And your lack of argument, the lack of a comeback to what I've told you, says a whole lot more than you think. You believe him, simple as that—or you want to believe him. I don't want to be with you until you believe *me*. So until that time, I'll make myself scarce. As we discussed, when we have spats, it's best to take time apart." I paused with my hand on the doorknob. "Oh, and just so you know, *I'm* also prepared to have *you* in my life after *you've* mistrusted *me*. I also love *you* that much."

Oh my goodness, where had this ballsy woman come from?

He threaded his hands through his hair.

*Say something. Please, Blake, turn around and say something.*

He didn't.

*Oh.*

"Before I forget, Connor also suggested he'd get pictures of me manipulated and show you I wasn't the right woman for you. I'll leave it to your imagination to know what he meant by that. I threw the coffee in his face at that point. And I'll admit, I wish it had been boiling oil. I detest him, detest what he's doing to us—and all because he's full of envy. And he implied he'd kill me—like he implied he'd already tried to kill you. He brushed that off as nothing, by the way. Do what you will with that information, but I'm not safe here, not with him on the loose."

Still no response. I wasn't going to beat myself up over it. Blake was the kind of man who needed time. His trust issues ran incredibly deep. I was glad that I'd grown up enough the past year to realise that. Time, that's what he needed.

And I had enough work to do to keep my mind occupied while waiting for him.

"I'll hopefully be seeing you soon, then," I said, opening the door.

"I love you, Herman."

"I know you do."

Then I walked out of the room, closed the door quietly, and took the stairs as slowly as I could in case he came flying out behind me. To call me back. To beg my forgiveness for not having complete faith in me.

He didn't.

Down in the lobby at the bottom of the steps, I took a deep breath, relieved the receptionist wasn't behind the desk. I held back tears and wondered how I was going to get through the radio set with a smiley, happy voice. It was all very well being professional and blundering on regardless of what was going on in my life and inside me, but this would be my biggest challenge yet.

"You absolute *moron*!" Ginger shouted.

A spark of fear quickly ignited anger in my belly, and I turned around to give him all the hurt I was feeling inside by way of opening my mouth and letting it all stream out. He stood at the back of the foyer, face centimetres from a young blonde woman's, his cheeks red and one fist pulled back level with his shoulder.

Oh no. *No* way. He was *not* going to hit her.

I parted my lips to shout at him.

"You did *what*?" he snarled, spittle flying.

"I just told you. I flagged up an anomaly." The woman backed away to the wall, her hands fluttering as she brought them up in front of her to ward him off. "I told you about it before but you wouldn't listen."

Ginger lowered his fist, moving even closer to her. She held her hands up, keeping space between them.

"And what did I tell you at that time?" he asked, voice rigid with anger.

"That if I flagged something it would alert Blake and worry him unnecessarily. That you would take care of it."

"Sir. Where's the sir on the end of that sentence?" he asked. "I'm your superior, you little bitch, and don't you forget it. I'm effectively your boss, and going against your boss is a bad move in my book."

She drew in a shaky breath then let it out. "No, *Mr Hudson* is my boss. I've never forgotten that, which is more than I can say for you."

I slunk into a corner behind me so if Ginger turned he wouldn't immediately catch me listening. My heart thudded so hard I thought he'd hear it, and my chest tightened with fear for the woman. I had a feeling that if he punched her, I'd spring into action in a millisecond.

"You have a smart mouth, lady." He stared at her, eyes bulging, a shine forming on his face from where sweat had suddenly popped out.

"I have a smart mind too—enough to figure out what you're doing." She lifted her chin and narrowed her eyes. "Go ahead. Hit me. Then I'll also have that to add to my complaints when I go up and speak to Blake."

"Complaints?" he asked in a low voice. "So what else have you cooked up about me? Come on, tell me. Maybe it'll make me laugh so I don't end up giving you a whole new look with my fist when you're walking down that dark alley you take on your way home from work."

*Oh my God!*

I glanced up the stairs. Blake's office door was closed. If only he could hear what his precious brother was saying. I was torn between leaving this woman at Ginger's mercy, going to get Blake, or using my phone to say there was an emergency.

"So it was *you* following me every night?" she whispered. She shook her head, incomprehension written all over her face. "Wasn't it enough that I told you I didn't want to have sex with you? And wasn't my threat of telling Blake about you touching me inappropriately enough either?" She darted her eyes to the space above the main front door.

I did the same and spotted a camera. Everything would be recorded. For her sake I hoped that included sound. And if it didn't, I'd testify on her behalf if she needed me. This man had to be taught he couldn't ride roughshod over people.

"You're a worthless, no-dick wonder," she said then laughed in his face.

She was either insane for pushing his buttons or knew exactly what she was doing. I admired her courage and her determination to fight for what was right.

He shook his head, as though he couldn't get his head around what she'd had the nerve to say. "You…you just watch your back, d'you hear me? Keep your mouth shut—about everything, all of it, otherwise you'll find out I haven't even started playing dirty yet."

He stalked off, shoving through the front door and out onto the street. I watched him run across the road, dodging cars and taxis, then he disappeared into a bank. What was he up to now? Transferring all that stolen money somewhere? Into one of those secret banks on an island?

I walked out from my hiding space, going towards the woman slowly in case she was freaking out inside. I didn't want to give her another fright. She spotted me and widened her eyes, sliding sideways along the wall, as if she needed to get away from me.

I held a hand out. "It's okay. I heard everything. And I already know about the money, what he's been doing."

"Oh, thank God!" She sagged, her knees bending, her body sliding down the wall until she sat on the tiled floor. "This has been an utter nightmare."

I felt sorry for her, but she needed to save the meltdown until later.

"Get up," I said, sterner than I'd intended.

But it did the trick. She got to her shaky feet, breathing fast, and lifted a hand to her chest.

"He's gone into that bank over there," I said. "So go upstairs and tell Blake everything. I've tried, but he's having a hard time thinking his brother isn't as hot on family values as he is. If *you* report Connor, maybe Blake will finally listen."

"I flagged…" She closed her eyes. Tears spilled onto her cheeks.

"I heard. But that might not be enough. If you've spotted the trail, the way Connor's been doing it… Blake needs that kind of proof, otherwise Connor will just wave it away with excuses. He's got to have them ready—who wouldn't have a back-up plan for if things went wrong?"

"I have everything. Documents, lots of things. I've been collecting it all for months." She opened her eyes and straightened her spine. "I can do this."

"You can." *Please do this. Please make Blake see.*

I watched her walk away to the stairs then followed, waiting at the bottom as she climbed them. She went into the accounting room then returned with a beige folder. At Blake's door, she knocked, turning to look down at me.

I gave her the thumbs up and, as she disappeared into his office, I left the building, hurrying past the bank and hoping Ginger hadn't see me fly by.

# 22

**Diary**

**So Long Happy Ever After!**

I feel that I've done all I can. Been more than reasonable. That ugly, sneaky ginger little ferret may ultimately get the better of me, but at least I can hold my head high and know that I've told the truth, been honest and sincere. The rest is up to Blake. How somebody can be so blinded by the thought of a fake family façade baffles me. Ginger has snake written all over his speckled face.

I want to cancel all of my commitments in London and enrol on the mission to out that rat! Become Miss Marple for a few weeks, although DI Taylor hasn't done badly so far. I could conjure up piles of evidence and put him in jail where he belongs. Then Blake and I could continue in our eternal bliss.

But unfortunately I've been overtaken by a new, mature, responsible side of myself, which is reminding me again that if Blake doesn't find out for himself he will forever doubt me. Anything I try to tell him now is tainted because of his past experiences, and I need to let him do some digging of his own and hopefully discover the truth.

Maybe my new ally (secretary) can shed some light on the paperwork side of things. Show him some unruly figures that he can't ignore. Anything to help my case right now is necessity!

But even then, will he ever be able to come to terms with the truth? Will he ever be able to cut the cord from his brother and move forward without him?

What have I done? Why didn't I just say I'd lied and pretended nothing had happened while I was at Ginger's? Blake said he'd still love me even if I'd lied. Why did I get all moral and mature? I've ruined it all with wanting him to see that I matter, that how I feel is important. And I do, I am. That was the whole point of walking out of his office like that.

How does anyone choose between family and their girlfriend? Surely family always wins?

You idiot, Charlotte. Well done!

Goodbye happily ever after! Hello London, alone, again!

Being back in London had its plus points. In between jobs, I could cry into heaps of tissues without anyone seeing me. And miss Blake, wailing to myself about losing him if he didn't call me soon and let me know what was going on. Which was exactly what I'd been doing since my return. Thankfully, the radio session in New York had gone well. I'd only been required to chat for five minutes then sing a couple of songs, so it had been easy to switch into Lola mode and forget, for a short while, what had happened previously.

But I could cry a river after work in bed each night then, as the days passed, I'd make it back to safer shores.

Despite my recent diary entry, something inside me said that I'd done the right thing in standing up for myself and leaving Blake to find out what Ginger was really like on his own. He didn't need me around, giving him I-told-you-so looks. My man had a lot to deal with, financially and emotionally, and licking his wounds was better done without me there.

It didn't stop me wondering why he hadn't called me, though. I'd been home for two days and still no word. It brought back memories of last time, but he'd been in hospital then after that fall when Ginger hadn't bothered letting me know.

I'd give it a week then call Blake to see how he was doing. I wouldn't mention Ginger at all, just chat as though that nasty man didn't exist. If Blake chose to bring the subject up, so be it, but I was determined to act sensibly this time around.

Crying a lot meant exhaustion, and my goodness, I was exhausted this afternoon. I'd spent the past few hours on a morning chat show, talking on their sofa then singing at the end. I'd come home to have a little rest and found I'd run out of Phish Food, and no wallow session was complete without it. I planned a couple more hours of self-pity between jobs before getting back into Lola mode and moving along.

In my bedroom, I slung on a tracksuit, planning a quick dash into the corner shop to get the ice cream, no looking up, no eye contact, not even saying thanks to the cashier, to get out and back to the wallowing spot. Interaction with people wasn't on my priority list at the moment, so the quicker I went on this little jaunt, the better.

I made it to the shop in super-quick time, walking with my head down, attention on the pavement. Inside, I passed everything, going straight to the freezer, picking up the Phish then marching to the till.

Error.

Magazines and papers, always stacked so neatly by the tills, grabbed my attention. After all, I'd been working so hard and had no idea what was going on in the world outside my Lola bubble. I spotted a picture of myself on the cover of *Kiss Me* magazine and it brought me a calming sense that David was working hard on my behalf, even after I'd shouted at him back in New York. He hadn't contacted me since I'd got back other than by email to tell me my latest UK itinerary, and I knew, once Wallow Time was over, I needed to get hold of him in person and put our spat behind us. We couldn't work together with that loitering between us.

Someone came into the shop, so I put my head back down, only to spy a picture of Blake on the front of some tabloid newspaper. My stomach did somersaults. My emotions went haywire—oh my, I loved him. I grabbed the paper, paid for my things, then left the shop in the biggest hurry ever.

On my two-minute walk back to my house, a million thoughts ran through my head. Maybe Blake had sold a story about me. I could see the headline now. *Evil Cow Breaks Eligible Bachelor's Heart.*

I had to get home fast and read it.

In my living room, I tossed my handbag onto the sofa then sat with the blue-and-white plastic shopping bag down by my feet. I closed my eyes and reached blindly for it, dreading what the article said. I wanted to read it yet I didn't.

Oh, who was I kidding? I was dying to read it, bad news or not. At least then I'd know where I stood.

I pulled the paper from the bag. It took what felt like an hour to open my eyes. I lifted the paper then scanned the headline.

*Lola's Lover, New York's Nicest Businessman, Caught up in Vicious Lawsuit!*

*Oh my goodness.*

In smaller print beneath, it read, *Blake Hudson Sues Brother for Fraud!*

Everything had come to light, then. So why hadn't Blake called me already? Was he angry with me for forcing it on him to accept that his brother was a conniving, ginger little git? Was he struggling to come to terms with it all, maybe realising he'd known all along yet had refused to admit it to himself? That kind of betrayal was immense, and I could only imagine the pain he was going through. Which made me want to be there for him, to comfort and make him feel better. But perhaps he needed a bit more time. Perhaps he was in Wallow World too? Or was time zipping by for him, with lawyer meetings and whatever else went with this kind of accusation? And did that mean Ginger was in jail? I didn't know how these things worked, but he deserved to be, I knew that much. And I hoped that blonde accounting assistant had filed charges too. He shouldn't be around women, they weren't safe when he was near.

Plus, there was that little question of pride. If Blake called, he'd have to admit, even if he didn't say it outright, that I had been right and he'd been wrong. That Ginger was the liar, not me. Maybe he wasn't ready for that kind of confession yet. And that was okay, I truly understood how he might be feeling there – upset, embarrassed, ashamed that he'd leant more towards Ginger. And who could blame him? He'd known Ginger all his life. While I…

I read the rest of the article.

*Connor Beasley, head accountant for Hudson Enterprises, has been sued by Blake Hudson after an employee and a close friend of Hudson brought proof of fraud to his attention.*

Close friend? Was that me or someone else?

*Beasley, currently in for questioning, denies the allegations, but an anonymous source close to the family said with proof stacking up against him, "…Connor hasn't got a leg to stand on."*

*Last year, Hudson was in the limelight regarding another case of fraud – it seems the man is far too trusting when it comes to his money. Our source said, "This guy is amazing. He gives so much to charity and spreads his wealth far and wide, including being generous to his family, so I don't understand why Connor got greedy and wanted more. He has enough wealth of his own, thanks to Blake."*

*But that's the million-dollar question, isn't it? Why would a man scam his more-than-generous brother?*

*"Well, that's easy to answer," our source said. "Connor's greedy, always has been, and he's jealous of Blake. The amount of times I've seen Connor's envy written all over his face – I could fill a book with them."*

*Our source went on to say, "Blake doesn't deserve this. Connor, on the other hand, deserves to rot in jail for what he's done. And not just to Blake, either."*

*We asked for even more information, but our source wasn't prepared to provide it. However, we don't put out a story without digging for facts hidden deep inside closets, so our super sleuth, Patty Flint, went on a mission. A source, who prefers not to give her name at this time, claims he sexually harassed her. Now that, folks, is mighty disturbing. She has filed charges and we'll report on that as soon as we get new information.*

*Check us out on the Internet for more on this as the story develops. Remember, we're* Live Online, *giving you news the second it hits our desks!*

I flopped back against the sofa, wondering who the source close to the family was. Maybe friends of the Beasley's had known what Ginger was like for years. Blake might be the only one who couldn't fully see it—or just didn't want to accept it. But I could hardly believe that. He'd told me he knew what his brother's traits were.

This was all so…unbelievable. Okay, I'd known that the blonde accounts assistant was going to tell Blake, but for Blake to actually sue Ginger? His own brother? The pain of discovering what Ginger had done must have sliced Blake deep. Would I be able to sue Jenna?

*But she's my real sister…*

Did that matter?

I didn't want to contemplate ever being in Blake's shoes. I couldn't imagine Jenna doing the same thing to me, even if she had access to my bank and financial dealings. She just wouldn't do it.

I had a thought. The newspaper would have been plopped on the shelf around mid-afternoon at the latest. Something else could have developed by now. I slung the paper down then reached for my laptop from the coffee table. I booted up and accessed the news site, clicking the *Live Online* button then scanned the text for a headline mentioning Blake. I found one with Beasley in it instead.

*Breaking News… Beasley Admits Fraud After Bank Accounts Prove Deception!*

Satisfaction poured into me. Although Blake would be hurting, I was glad this had been brought out in the open. Ginger deserved to be dragged through the courts and be made to pay for what he'd done, but I had a feeling Blake would drop the charges. I realised Blake's money would never be recovered—not the amounts Ginger had already spent, anyway—but a prison sentence and the whole world knowing what a little ginger shit he was made happiness bubble up inside me.

I glanced at my phone, desperate to call Blake.

*No, leave it. Give him time. Let him come to you.*

I continued to read the new information.

*Patty Flint, our female version of Columbo, has been out again with her trusty spade, digging and piling up a whole heap of dirt. It has come to light that Connor Beasley, former head accountant at Hudson Enterprises, has allegedly rerouted in excess of six million dollars into his personal accounts.*

Live Online *will update as soon as anything new comes in. Stay tuned!*

I could kiss Patty Flint, whoever she was, for going after Ginger the way she had. But not for the hurt her findings would cause Blake and the Beasley family. From what Blake had told me, they were a lovely bunch of people, so to have this happening had to have been a vicious blow.

I closed my laptop with mixed feelings. I wasn't about to deny that Ginger had got his just desserts, and that I'd been vindicated. I just wished this could all have been done quietly, instead of it being a media circus. But it would have been Blake's decision to sue, knowing this kind of news would be big.

Had he done it to show me he believed me? To safeguard me from being hurt by Ginger—really hurt? Was I being conceited in thinking that?

Whatever the reason, what was done was done, and I really felt the need for company. Sitting here by myself with ice cream didn't seem so appealing now.

*I must put that Phish in the freezer before it melts.*

I thought of the only person I ever turned to in the most dreadful times of crisis. The one who knew all my secrets and never told a soul. I hadn't seen him for what felt like ages, and a good dose of his high spirits and simple way of looking at things would put stuff in perspective. I hadn't emailed him much lately and, true to form, he'd given me the space I'd needed to get on with work. He'd left me alone after telling me he'd found the love of his life and he'd be busy without me anyway. He'd also said he had big news, something he had to tell me in person, and that it could wait until I got back to the UK.

Well, I was back, so he could tell me now.

Yes, he was what I needed. Grabbing my bag then slinging it over my shoulder, I marched to the front door. For the first time in too many hours, I was ready to get back out there and start living again.

I was off to see Roo-Roo, my wonderful gay best friend.

# 23

I made it to Rupert's one-storey inside ten minutes, arriving on his doorstep out of breath and desperate to tell him everything that had been going on. His advice was always invaluable, and I looked forward to hearing it. He'd clear my head of all the dark murk and put sunshine there instead, helping me to see what I hadn't been able to so far.

I banged on the door with the side of my fist, eager for him to open it quickly. He was in—his living room light seeped out past the closed curtains, and that gave me pause to stop hammering. He never usually closed his curtains.

"Please answer, Rupert, I need you. It's me, Charlotte!"

I heard a muffled, "Oh, sodding heck!" then saw a silhouette coming towards the mottled glass in the door. Had he stubbed his toe or something?

It felt like forever for him to open the door, but when he swung it back, he stood in his hallway looking flustered. And he was half naked. That didn't bother me. I flounced in without waiting for him to invite me, shutting the door then flinging myself into his arms.

"Oh, Roo-Roo, you would not believe the stuff that's been happening!" I said, wondering why he didn't wrap his arms around me like he normally would. I pulled back to stare at his face.

He was grimacing and seemed uncomfortable. What on earth was wrong with him?

"Oh, my darling petal," he said, "I've missed you, but…"

Phew, there was the answer I'd wanted. "My goodness, I need wine. Do you have wine? I want lots of it. And a blanket, so I can curl up on the sofa with you and let you know all the nonsense going on in my life. I'm telling you, this love business is so difficult sometimes!" I let him go and made my way into his kitchen.

I turned to give him one of my eye-rolls, only to find he hadn't followed me. He was still in the hallway, gazing across at his bedroom door.

"Oh," I said, realising I'd arrived unannounced and had maybe caught him entertaining the new boyfriend. "I am soooo sorry. I didn't realise. I just needed a friend and… I should have thought. I should have called first. I'm just so used to you being there at all hours." I smiled apologetically. "So who's the lucky guy?"

Rupert didn't answer.

I felt totally awkward, as though I shouldn't be there. "I'll, um, I'll just go. I can catch up with you another time, all right?"

Rupert nodded, still not looking at me. So was he nodding at the boyfriend? He whispered something I couldn't catch. I stepped forward to join him but he squealed, holding his hand up to stop me going any farther.

"Uh, let me just…" He shrugged. "There's something I need to tell you. I said that in my last email, didn't I, darling? But I don't think now's the right time for it. So, er, if you could wait a second while…" He glanced at his bedroom door again, making shooing movements with his other hand at whoever was in there. "Go! *Go*!"

Oh, this was silly. Was his boyfriend shy, was that it? Or was it someone I knew and he didn't want me to see him? Perhaps he hadn't come out of the closet yet, but that was okay, Rupert knew I could keep a secret like that. We told each other everything. Or almost everything.

I strode out into the hall.

And saw Jenna standing in the bedroom doorway, a sheet wrapped around her.

*Jenna?*

*At Rupert's?*

Had they made friends while I'd been in New York? Her blonde hair was ruffled every which way, as though she'd been asleep, fighting demons in a nightmare. Had another resident at the old people's home died again and she'd needed some support? I wouldn't put it past Rupert to have contacted her while I was away, knowing I wouldn't have time to be my usual support to her. The thought of him doing that for my sister brought on a huge smile of gratitude.

Then another thought hit me. What if she *was* upset, and there was me, smiling my head off? She looked shocked that I was there, and tired, as though she hadn't slept for days. Okay, I hadn't told her or Dad that I was back in the UK yet, but that wasn't cause for her to stare at me that way.

"What's the matter?" I rushed to the bedroom to grab her into a hug.

She rested her chin on my shoulder and hugged me back. "I'm sorry."

"What for?" I asked and eased back so I could see her face. "Did something happen while I was gone? Is Dad all right?" My heart took that second to thunder, hard and fast and mean, and panic chased away any thoughts I'd had of blurting all my news out to Rupert. Goodness, I was so unthinking at times.

"No, no, it's not Dad. He's fine, just missing your cups of tea." She gave me a watery smile.

"Then what is it?" I turned to look over my shoulder at Rupert, who stood there in just a pair of boxer shorts.

*Boxer shorts.*

*Jenna's mussed up and standing there in a sheet.*

Rupert looked tired too, like he hadn't slept for days either.

No. Surely not. Roo-Roo was *gay,* for goodness sake. Unless he was bi and hadn't said?

My jaw dropped. Realisation started hitting me, way too hard and way too fast. I'd never actually *seen* Rupert with another man. I'd assumed he was gay because of how he acted. Everyone I knew had assumed it too.

Then I remembered what he'd said to me one time last year.

*'I'm one person with everyone else and myself with me.'*

Had he been trying to tell me something? Had he been acting gay all this time, or was he generally just an exuberant man?

"Do you remember that time, petal?" he asked.

He knew me so well, knew what I was thinking. I nodded.

"What you saw was me, the way I am, and people assumed something else so I let them." He smiled sadly.

"But like I told you, I was myself when alone, and I had no idea I'd ever find anyone who saw past the craziness, my mad behaviour, to who I really am. But Jenna..." He gave her a longing glance. "I bumped into her at the care home—my nan's in there now, sweetie—and she saw me. The real me. Said she had from the first day she'd met me when you'd taken me over to your dad's that time. And... It went from there." He sighed, the exhalation shaky. "Are you angry with me? With us?"

Angry? Only at myself for not realising sooner. I'd been so wrapped up in me and my world since I'd met Rupert, clinging onto him as a friend, and him showing me the ropes and holding my hand at parties, that I'd failed the BFF test appallingly. Which squashed any thoughts on why Rupert hadn't told me the truth. Maybe he felt he didn't need to, that his love life wasn't something we had to discuss in great detail. And we hadn't. As far as I was concerned, he could go to bed with whoever he liked. Gay had never been an issue.

"Bloody hell, no!" I said, hugging Jenna tighter and rocking her from side to side. "How can I be angry that two of my best friends are together?"

His smile changed his worried expression, showing his relief. "Things aren't always as they seem, darling. It's a tough old world out there and you gotta do what you gotta do to survive, right?"

I knew exactly what he meant too. He'd been embraced by celebs because of his amazing personality and his brilliant makeup skills, nothing more, nothing less.

"I can't think of a better man for you, Jenna." I relaxed my hold on her so the poor woman could actually breathe. I smiled at Rupert. "Or a better woman for you." Overcome with emotion, I blinked away tears.

I needed to leave them to it, without spewing out my troubles. They were in the first flush of love and didn't need me tainting it with my woes. It wasn't so long ago that I had been with Blake, thinking of nothing but him—being with him, laughing with him, planning the rest of my life with him. And seeing Jenna and Rupert staring across at each other now gave me the kick up the backside I needed.

I had to contact Blake.

I let Jenna go and moved towards the front door.

"Where are you going, missus?" Rupert asked, hands on hips, lips pursed.

I laughed—he was such a fun man.

"I'm going home. You two… I think I interrupted something." I winked.

He clucked his tongue. "Well, if you really want to know—"

"Uh, no, I don't." I raised my hand. "Not this time. We share many things, but not that. Please, not that!" I laughed, stealing one of his gestures and holding the back of my hand up to my forehead.

Jenna shuffled away from the bedroom doorway. "But when you arrived you said you needed to talk. And that you need wine. We have wine, so talk."

It was so tempting to open up to these two at the same time. It would save me repeating myself but… Could I dump it all on them when they were so happy, so loved-up?

"Please do," Rupert said. "We could do with a…break."

"Are you sure?" I stared from him to Jenna.

"We're sure," Jenna said. "Let me just fling on some clothes and I'll meet you in the living room."

Rupert grinned. "I, on the other hand, will converse with you in my underpants. After all, why change just because I'm with your sister?"

I laughed, and it felt so good. I walked into the kitchen to grab a bottle of wine and three glasses while Jenna went to get changed. In the living room, I handed Rupert the corkscrew then placed everything else on his coffee table.

"You're sure you don't find this weird, petal?" he asked.

"A bit, but only because I thought…"

"So the fact that it's Jenna is okay?"

He looked so worried I tugged him forward for a cuddle.

"Shut it." I knuckled the top of his head. "If you're with your soulmate, then I'm not going to stand in your way. Besides, I'm looking at this from a purely selfish standpoint. Both of my rocks are combined. Now the pair of you are a force that no one will reckon with. And you're on my team. I couldn't ask for a better duo to have my back."

"Oh, we had your back before we got together," he said, voice muffled while I continued messing his hair. "And will you get off me, you bloody bully! Jenna! Help! Your sister's picking on me!"

I laughed again, stepping back and away just as Jenna walked in. "What? I didn't do anything. He's making it up."

She knew me too well and I knew she'd join me in ribbing him.

"Rupert, don't make lies up about my sister," she said. "I won't believe a negative word you say about her."

That brought me up short. Reminders of why I was here slapped me hard, and the smile dropped from my face. Blake. Ginger. Everything.

"Oh, what's wrong?" Jenna came towards me with her hand out.

"It's okay." I gave her a wobbly smile. "I'll be all right. It was just something you said."

Rupert tilted his head. "Oh, this is cause for lots of wine. More than one bottle, I can tell. Sit down, darling." He waved a hand at the sofa behind me. "And tell Roo-Roo and Jenna all about it."

I did, blathering on between sips of wine until I was out of breath and had no energy left to continue. Exhaustion swamped me again, and I curled my legs up beneath me so I became a little ball in the corner.

"Oh no, don't you *dare* do that." Rupert wagged a finger at me. "From what you've said, striking that defeatist pose is *not* who you are anymore. Days gone by, yes, we've sat here and been hermits, thrashing out our troubles until we passed out from too much alcohol, but not anymore. I have my soulmate and you have yours. Okay, there's yet another glitch in your path to happiness, but…" He slapped my knee. "Do I need to remind you it was me who prodded you to contact him first the last time you had a big misunderstanding? Do I need to do it again?"

"No, I was going to get hold of him when I left here anyway, but talking about it all just now…" I drank some more wine. "I slipped back into the old Charlotte mode."

"So slip back out of it," Jenna said. "Ring him up. Yes, he's bound to have been busy the past couple of days, what with the lawsuit and everything, but that's long enough. You need to check in, let him know you're still there for him." She canted her head to one side. "Look at it this way—what if he thinks you just left him? I mean, I know you said you made it clear you were coming back here to give him space, but what if he took that literally? As in, space forever?"

"And," Rupert added, "what if he feels such a loser, for not fully believing you, that he can't bring himself to call you just yet? Why not make it easier for him? Save him some agony while you're at it. The poor boy could be torturing himself with guilt over this. He made you think he believed that horrid ginger person and not you. He's got to be feeling pretty bad about that, don't you think?"

I had to agree. And I'd already told Blake I understood why he'd be torn between me and Ginger, but that might not make any difference to how he felt now.

"And what about this?" Rupert poured himself some more wine then added a splash or two to our glasses. "What if he actually *knew* deep down Ginger Boy was capable of such things? You said yourself he suspected something about the accident. And you couldn't see Blake's face when you blurted out your thing. What if his mind was racing with all that information and he didn't think you'd really hop on a plane back here? He could have gone home, thinking you'd be there, and found you gone. He probably feels all kinds of pig for that, dear."

A sudden urge to see Blake *right now* hit me. I was glad I hadn't had more than one helping of wine and that I had time before my next UK job to do what I had in mind. I stood, plonking my glass on the table, and walked to the living room door.

"I can't thank you both enough for everything you've ever done for me, but I have to go. I love you – and enjoy getting to know one another."

I rushed to the front door.

"Let us know when you get home," Rupert called. "Give us a text."

"I will," I shouted. "But I won't be home long enough to send anything more than 'OK!'."

"What do you *mean*, petal?" Rupert appeared in the living room doorway, a frown firmly in place, his cheeks flushed from wine.

"I'm going to follow your advice. How can the two most sure and honest people in my life ever be wrong? But I'm not going to text or call him." I smiled as I opened the door. "I'm going to go to New York to see him in person."

# 24

## Diary

### Flying on Determination

My sister and my best friend! What a pleasant yet awkward surprise. I've got it made in the supportive friends department. A force of great advice and laughter. GOALS! I am officially winning.

I can't believe I'm already on this flight to The Big Apple! How did I get here? I feel like I've only just landed back in London.

Pretty underwear, check.

I'm-back-and-I-love-you outfit, check.

Balls, check.

I'm ready to do this. I need him to know I haven't just left him in the lurch. We *can* do this together, united!

Sugar. Note to self—must call David the minute I touchdown and let him know, before he has a heart attack when he calls me and the dialling tone is international. He'll understand, even though I've hardly had any contact with him since our little spat.

Oh no! No, don't worry, just get yourself off of this plane, Charlotte, and think sensibly later. I hope he hasn't grown resentment towards me for leaving.

I just want to grab the air hostess for one of those girlie BFF chats I've been longing for. Tell her what I'm doing in an attempt to get some reassurance of what a great girlfriend I am and how I'm doing the right thing.

This is the longest seven and a half hours of my life. Sleep brain sleep!

Standing on American soil so soon after I'd left it felt surreal. My body clock had only just started getting back to normal two days after landing in London, and now I was messing it up all over again. I'd slept a little on the plane, drifting in and out of slumber that had been interrupted by dreams born of insecurity. The usual thing—what if he didn't want me back? What if he couldn't cope with the fact I'd ruined his happy family? What if all the hurt and suffering Blake and the Beasleys were going through was too much for him for forgive?

Then I thought about it rationally—I was getting better at doing that!—and told myself that what would be would be. If he told me to sling my hook, I would. Okay, I'd beg him to see sense and understand that I'd told him everything because I couldn't just let Ginger scam him for the rest of his life, but if he wouldn't accept my explanation, then that was that.

Words to describe the fallout of that? Heartbroken. Devastated. One crushed half of a whole. I didn't need any more. Those few summed it up perfectly.

I'd landed at eleven a.m., and by the time I'd gone through the security checks and pushed my way out of a busy JFK and onto the pavement to hail a taxi, I was getting travel weary. I fought fatigue, pushing myself to book into a hotel, dump my case—I hadn't unpacked it from before—and leg it down the street to Blake's office building.

I staggered into the foyer, remembering how I'd felt the last time I'd walked through that door, and headed for the stairs.

"Excuse me! Charlotte, isn't it?" the receptionist asked.

I ignored her, dragging my lethargic body up the stairs then giving Blake's door a token polite knock before going inside. The room was empty, and I sagged against the frame, desperate to speak to him, thinking fate was playing one of her silly little games again by making me work for my happiness.

"Um, hello?" the receptionist called.

I turned to look down the stairs. She stood at the bottom, hands on hips, her pursed mouth resembling an animal's bumhole. I was so tired I wanted to laugh but the energy for it had deserted me.

"Where's Mr Hudson?" I asked, going down the steps to stand beside her. "I have to see him immediately."

"He's at his lawyer's office, but I have orders not to disturb him for obvious reasons." She folded her arms across her tummy.

"Right." I took the stairs again with renewed vigour. "I'll just wait up here, then."

"Oh, but… I think you should wait down here! It really isn't—"

"It's okay, he won't mind!" I darted inside his office then slapped my back against the door to catch my breath. I waited for the receptionist to try storming in but a couple of minutes passed without her appearing so I breathed easier.

Launching myself off the door and to his desk, I ferreted in his filing cabinet until I found what I needed. No one could accuse me in this case of not being single-minded in order to get what I wanted. His lawyer's office was a block away, apparently, and although I could have taken a taxi, I estimated I'd probably get there faster on foot by the time a cab arrived.

Back in the foyer, I made for the front door. "You're right." I smiled at the receptionist. "I'll wait outside."

"Oh, there's no need for that," she said from behind her desk. "There's a sofa right here."

I wanted to laugh again. The desk was so high she was just a disembodied head. The tiredness of the past couple of days was getting to me.

"No, no, I need some fresh air."

Off I went, gallivanting down the street, the chill in the air spurring me faster as it did its best to freeze the skin off my face. I felt like a speed runner, all willpower and guts of steel to win the race, and blundered on, all thoughts of what I'd say to Blake if I caught up with him vanishing from my mind. Maybe that was for the best. Plotting the way the conversation would go rarely ended up the way I expected, anyway.

I rounded a corner and pushed on, frowning as I spotted a crowd gathered halfway down the street. I got closer and realised it was the lawyer's office and the people were the press. With no time to lose—surely them being there meant Blake was still inside—I sped on, my lungs burning and my legs protesting. If muscles could scream obscenities, mine would be shouting all kinds of bad words.

I stood at the edge of the crowd.

And then the news teams and photographers flocked forward in one swarming, mad rush to the entrance.

*Here he comes! It's got to be him they're here for.*

Excitement flushed my system, leaving me lightheaded and weak in the knees. I was about to clap eyes on the love of my life, and if he didn't want to clap eyes on me, I'd soon see. And so would the cameras and people around me, but I was past caring what anyone else thought now. I wanted my man. I wanted to tell him I loved him, for him to hold me in his arms and swirl me around, madman fashion. I wanted to let him know that he'd done the right thing, that I didn't care he'd seemingly taken Ginger's word over mine. We'd get over that, tuck it into the past where it belonged, and move forward to a brighter, happier future.

Oh, and there he was, a vision of perfection. All I could make out was the top of his head, his beautiful hair and his furrowed brow, but that was okay, better than seeing nothing at all. It seemed the hustle and commotion, the jostle of the crowd, the shouted questions…all of it vanished and it was just me and Blake. Everything went silent, and he walked away from the crowd to stand on the top step.

My slow-mo vision and lack of hearing were broken by the sound of an enthusiastic reporter ready to get the first quote.

"How does it feel knowing someone who's been like a brother could be going to jail and that you sent him there?"

"No comment," said a small, bald man beside Blake. He looked like someone not to be messed with. "Please have some respect here!"

*Sod respect!*

I elbowed my way through the crowd, not caring that I jabbed some poor bloke in the cheek. No one was stopping me from getting to my Mr Perfect. Blake had his head down and was trying to push past the ever-crushing throng, but they were having none of it. They surged closer until he was pressed against the building, his lawyer squashed at his side.

"Blake!" I shouted.

He snapped his head up, scanning the crowd, blinking as though he thought he'd imagined my voice.

"Give the man some room," the lawyer yelled, managing to prise himself away from Blake and bat at some of the more aggressive news crews.

"I'm here! Blake!"

I went up on tiptoes, waving my arms above my head, grinning madly and wishing these people would just bugger off out of my way.

"Move, will you?" I snarled at those near me, and I must have sounded ferocious because they shifted, creating a looser melee, one I could navigate more easily.

Blake spotted me, and for a millisecond a smile ripped into his face before he schooled his features into a blank expression.

*Oh, he doesn't want me here.*

*Well, that's just tough. I am here and I'm not leaving until I say what I've got to say.*

Bolstered by my determination, I barrelled through the people until I stood in a small space at the bottom of the steps. The crowd seemed to have sensed something newsworthy other than the case and eased back, creating a path from the bottom step to the top.

"It's Lola!" someone whispered.

Blake began walking down the steps.

*Oh my God. Oh my God…*

He frowned. Frowned even deeper.

I held my breath.

He stopped right in front of me.

Tears welled up in my eyes at the sight of his cross face, and I waited for him to shoot me down right there and then.

He opened his mouth.

I let out my breath. Took another. Held it again.

"You should have been here sooner, Herman. What took you so long?"

He reached out, taking me by my upper arm, and tugged me to him. I stared up into his eyes, seeing he was still angry, thinking I had my answer—that I needed to hightail it back to London and forget all about him.

He lowered his head as though what he was about to say was for my ears only.

*He's going to tell me to go. That he doesn't want me…*

Blake crushed his lips to mine, and it took me a startled few seconds to realise what he was doing. I closed my eyes and slumped against him, suddenly conscious that I was still wearing my tracksuit from being in Wallow World. I could only imagine what a state I looked, but as his kiss grew deeper, I decided I didn't care if he didn't.

Tears came then, streaming uncontrollably as all of my suppressed emotions seemed to leave my body through my eyes. The relief of this latest visit to Hell being over made every muscle and bone in my body stop functioning. Blake held me up, kissing me harder, and didn't let go for what must have been a good minute or two. I was sure the news cameras were rolling, the photographers were snapping away, but that was fine by me.

Finally, he broke the kiss and, staring down at me, said, "I'm sorry. I should have called."

"No, I'm sorry, I should never have left."

"I'll never question you again," he whispered then ushered me back into the building.

With the door closed firmly against the crowd, I stared up into his eyes.

"From here on out, Herman, only trust, honesty and love."

I nodded – oh, how I nodded. "So what about right now?"

"Right now, we're going to go home."

"Where's home?" I asked, knowing it didn't matter where it was anymore. We were past all that, but still, I couldn't help but be curious.

He kissed me soundly again then drew me into his arms, crushing me tighter than he had before. "Here, here is where home is."

He didn't elaborate. He could have meant in his arms or here in New York. For now I just wanted to stay right where I was, basking in the warmth of his body, the strength of his arms.

But that little voice inside me wouldn't shut up and I resisted the urge to push him into giving me a definite answer.

"Have you been hiding out in a bush again?" He stroked my mad hair and eyed me up and down.

"No, but I have been to Wallow World."

"Say what?"

I laughed with crazy, wild abandon.

"I have something to show you," he said.

"You do?" I stared up at him and wondered what it could be.

"Hmm. But first I think you could do with some sleep."

I couldn't argue with that.

"So when you're refreshed, I'll take you there." He kissed the tip of my nose.

"Take me where?"

"Home. I'll take you home."

"But where *is* that?"

"Well, you'll just have to wait and see, won't you?"

# About the Author

The multi-talented Stacey Solomon was the X-Factor 2009's last standing female contestant after coming third in the show.

In late 2010, she entered ITV's I'm a Celebrity Get Me Out of Here and was crowned Queen of the Jungle. She was also voted Mum of the Year in 2011 and is currently the face of Look Again.

2015 saw Stacey release her first fiction novel, a new single and her own perfume.

Check out the series website for Best Things in Life at https://www.totallybound.com/celebritease/stacey-solomon

# More books from Totally Bound

A chick lit story to make you laugh out loud.

Carrie Sinclair thought she knew exactly what she wanted from life until she came face-to-face with the bluest eyes in Texas.

A beautiful, heart-wrenching story set in wartime Britain.

War puts courage and love to the test.

Sexy, fun and sweet. A feel-good romance.

Matchmaker extraordinaire Molly Matthews is an expert in love, but her skills are put to the ultimate test when international heartthrob Rory Campbell waltzes into her office.

A poignant contemporary romance.

When Nadine loses it all, she must rebuild her life. But maybe she no longer wants what she used to have.

TOTALLY BOUND

Home of Erotic Romance